First Fruits

A Novel

Bethany,

May your coffee may always be full and Steve not make things weird! And may Jesus bless you always! Stay awesome!

Brad D

By

Brad Duncan

First Printing, 2013

Bradleyjeep Publishing
ISBN # 978-0-9912858-0-8

© 2014 Compassion International name used with permission

Cover art by Jordan Mountjoy
Copyright 2013

Books may be purchased in quantity and/or special sales by contacting
www.3tChallenge.com

Acknowledgements

Thank you to all the men and women who have helped me grow in my faith in Jesus Christ. My mom and dad are the best parents I can imagine. My sister, Jamie, and I were very blessed to grow up in a Christian home, where we still knew how to have a great time and laugh like crazy. A special thanks to my beautiful, patient, loving wife, Michelle. She is a blessing words cannot express. My three girls, Maddie, Mackenzie, and Abby are my pride and joy. They are all three beautiful on the inside and out.

Chapter 1

Pastor Patrick Spakes looked across his sanctuary filled with more people than its pews could hold, and he was filled with pride. All the hard work, the countless phone calls, the expensive mail-outs, and the long evenings away from his family had paid off. There were so many people in attendance extra chairs had to be set up in the aisles. He looked out into the congregation and smiled at his lovely wife, Christy. She was sitting with their seventeen year old son, Daniel, and their fifteen year old daughter, Jamie. Christy smiled back thinking how happy he would be if today's goal was met.

"Just as I Am" was being half-heartedly sung by the massive gathering of people. No one was coming forward during the invitation, but that was of no concern to Pastor Patrick this morning. Success or failure on this day would be achieved simply by the number of people in attendance. This was High Attendance Sunday! The goal of five hundred people must be met, or all of the hard work and preparation would be a total and complete failure.

He prayed to himself, *Lord, you know how hard I've worked to get people here today. Please let us break the five hundred person mark this morning.* Just as he finished praying, Joe Smith, head of the Board of Deacons, entered the back of the sanctuary with an envelope in his hand. The pastor stepped forward, midway through the final verse of the song, raising his hand in the air to stop everything.

"It looks like we have the results for today's attendance! Come on up Deacon Joe. Two years ago we broke the two-hundred fifty person barrier. Last year we broke the four-hundred person mark. As you are all aware, this year's goal is to break five hundred!"

As the pastor spoke, Deacon Joe marched to the front of the church and handed him the envelope. Taking it he said, "I certainly hope this contains good news, Deacon Joe."

In a melancholy voice the deacon spoke for all to hear, "Well, Pastor, I know everyone did their best." He took his seat on the front row as the pastor opened the envelope and peeked at its contents.

Pastor Patrick noticeably slumped as if he had just received heart-breaking news. He shook his head from side to side for a moment. Then in a somber voice he said, "I know you all worked hard. We have counted everyone in here, all the kids in children's church, and in the nursery. Every soul counts. We did have a good turnout. Regardless if we break five hundred today or not, I know God is proud of you."

All eyes were transfixed on him and the envelope in his hand containing the results of their hard work.

They were all hoping the pastor's tell-tale signs of defeat were not true. The tension in the room was palpable and everyone was on the edge of their seat anticipating the pastor's next words. Pastor Patrick was naturally gifted in theatrics and this was a moment he loved.

"Today's official attendance at Big Oak Christian Church is..." then after pausing for dramatic effect he loudly proclaimed, "five hundred and three!"

A shout arose from the congregation as they exploded in a great chorus of cheering and clapping! Some people hugged. Some gave high fives. Some even cried.

Pastor Patrick, a smile now on his face from ear to ear, called for order.

"I'm so proud of every one of you. You should be proud of yourselves and of your church. Now, who thinks we can break seven hundred people next year?"

The congregation laughed and cheered. Christy Spakes was filled with mixed emotions. She was glad her husband had reached the goal he had worked so long and hard for. He had met the challenge he placed before himself once again. But the thought of already setting the attendance bar so high for next year made her feel tired and lonely. Maybe even a bit jealous of all the attention the church would receive at her expense. But for now, she would choose to be happy for him. The elated pastor dismissed the service with a short prayer thanking God for allowing them success in meeting their goal once again this year.

Toward the back of the sanctuary sat Sister Ruth Snyder. She was a spry woman in her nineties. Mentally she was sharp, and spiritually a prayer warrior second to none. As she sat watching the celebration, her spirit was troubled. She had learned over her many years of devotion to Jesus to be sensitive to the Holy Spirit.

Sister Snyder did not know it, but God was going to use her to deliver a pivotal message affecting every person attending Big Oak Christian Church; especially Pastor Patrick Spakes.

Chapter 2

Big Oak Christian Church, located in the city of Lost Creek, was no stranger to experiencing ups and downs. Seven years ago they had called a smooth talking preacher to lead them. Big Oak was a financially healthy church and was steadily growing at the time. This new preacher convinced enough of the people they needed to build a new elaborate church sanctuary they could ill afford. They did need the space, but not the luxurious amenities he desired.

One year after the sanctuary was complete, he was caught stealing from the church. Under a cloud of scandal he resigned and left town. His tenure left Big Oak with a luxurious four hundred seat sanctuary, a mountain of debt, and a dwindling congregation.

Pastor Patrick was called by Big Oak to try to restore the church back to viability. He loved the challenge. First, he restructured the huge loan from the local Lost Creek Bank. Second, he rallied the remaining members of Big Oak to believe in him and the church once again. Then he spent countless hours building relationships with church members, visiting prospective members, and restoring Big Oak's reputation in the community. He had brought Big Oak from the brink of collapse. She was once again a vibrant exciting church.

Sister Snyder was the matriarch of Big Oak Christian Church. Her father had started Big Oak when she was only five years old. She met Seth Snyder there. They grew up going to church together and fell in love. They were married in the church the same year Seth was ordained. He became the pastor of Big Oak a couple of years into their marriage. Seth pastored Big Oak for the next fifty years. The church was basically their family.

Like everyone who knew Sister Snyder, Pastor Patrick had no doubt she was a woman who loved Jesus with all her heart.

The story was she had a big influence on bringing him to Big Oak. It was somewhat hard to believe since he never felt like she respected him as a pastor. She would always tell him she was praying for him and his family. He felt this was her way of saying he was insufficient as a pastor in her eyes. Plus the fact she chose to call him "Brother" instead of "Pastor", like everyone else, added to his aggravation toward her.

As Sister Snyder approached him and his wife Christy, at the back of the church, he found himself hoping to receive some praise from her for the morning's great achievement. He would be disappointed.

Sister Snyder walked slowly to the pastor and his wife. She honestly didn't want to deliver this message while he was so obviously happy.

He smiled as she reached him and took her hand saying, "It's good to see you this morning, Sister! Isn't it great to see Big Oak filled up with so many souls?!" He was hoping this would coax her into acknowledging his hard work and success.

Sister Snyder replied, "I know how hard you have worked to build a big church here. I appreciate your effort. Brother Spakes, I have a word from the Lord I must share with you."

Pastor Patrick, laughing and smiling said, "By all means, Sister. Please tell me what you think God wants me to hear."

Sister Snyder replied, "1 Corinthians 3:11-13 and Exodus 23:19. Read those scriptures and know that God will work quickly. Pray and be ready to put your trust and faith in Him. I will be praying for you and your family."

The pastor flipped open his Bible and jotted down the scriptures on a scrap sheet of paper. He gave Sister Snyder a final smile and said, "Thank you for always praying for me. I'll definitely check out those scriptures." Once again he felt inadequate in her eyes. What was it about this old woman that made him feel like he was miles away from where he should be with God? He was torn between respect and resentment toward her.

It wouldn't be long before he would be searching for her wisdom and begging for her prayers.

Chapter 3

Pastor Patrick could not think of a more fitting place to celebrate today's success than Champion's Steakhouse. Deacon Joe had reserved the party room for the "post-game celebration" as he liked to call it. There were about sixty people squeezed in there from Big Oak, and they all clapped and cheered as the Spakes family entered the room.

Pastor Patrick held up his right hand for quiet and said triumphantly, "It's good to be a winner. Now, let's eat!"

Everyone roared with laughter. He worked the room like a seasoned politician, acknowledging everyone by name. Shaking hands with Sky Burleson he said, "Great song this morning. You and Chloe are undiscovered stars."

Sky and Chloe were both musically gifted and in love. They were engaged, and planned to be married in Big Oak's beautiful sanctuary the coming fall.

"Thanks Pastor! I just try not to mess things up for Chloe. She's the real talent," Sky said smiling.

Chloe blushed a bit, squeezed Sky's hand, and said, "He's a real charmer."

Christy interjected, "Well enjoy it sweetheart. In a few years you'll wonder where all that charm went!" They all laughed, including Christy who was only half-way kidding.

Pastor Patrick jokingly told one of the deacon's wives he would be in need of a nice long sabbatical soon. Christy, overhearing the remark, wanted to make him promise he would take some time off in front of all the influential leaders gathered here. That he would spend some time with her and the kids, nourishing what should be his most important relationships. But she knew it was just him rambling. Mere talk. A part of her felt guilty for being jealous of the Bride of Christ. But wasn't she his bride? Shouldn't he want to spend time with her too? Why did the church get his best while she got whatever was left over? She didn't want him to stop preaching. She just wanted to feel loved again. Christy pasted a smile on her face and took her seat by her husband.

He led a prayer of celebration for his merry group. Food was devoured and laughs were shared.

He jokingly said to the filled room, "Now don't forget to give your tithes. I might need a raise, since we're finally going to two services."

Deacon Joe replied, "We'll just videotape the first service and show it to the second. That way our church can spend its money on something other than you saying the same thing twice in one morning."

The crowd once again roared with laughter. Pastor Patrick and Deacon Joe's banter was famous around Big Oak's members. When Patrick became the pastor, the two men had quickly become friends. They both loved competition and success. Their sons, Daniel and JJ, which was short for Joe Jr., became best friends. They played high school baseball together and played for a summer tournament travel baseball team.

After the delicious meal, the Spakes were the last to leave. They made it home and Christy asked her husband, "Why don't you come lay down with me and rest? The kids won't be home until later. You've earned it."

He replied, "That sounds great, but I better call some of today's visitors first. You gotta ride the momentum while you got it!" Christy just smiled to hide her disappointment and went to lay down alone.

After an evening of calling visitors and thanking them for attending Big Oak, Pastor Patrick and Christy ate a bite and got ready for bed.

Christy asked, "Did you get a chance to check out those Bible verses Sister Snyder told you about?"

"Oh, I totally forgot. I'll check them out real quick," he replied. He went downstairs to his study and opened his Bible to the note the scriptures were scribbled upon.

Alright, he thought to himself, *let's see what Sister Snyder has for me. She certainly sounded worried about me seeing them.*

He read 1 Corinthians 3:11-13: "For no man can lay a foundation other than the one which is laid, which is Jesus Christ. Now if any man builds on the foundation with gold, silver, precious stones, wood, hay, straw, each man's work will become evident; for the day will show it because it is to be revealed with fire, and the fire itself will test the quality of each man's work."

Well that's not the most encouraging passage, he thought. *I guess she just doesn't like change. I can't really blame her. She's so old. Life must be tough at her age. I'll call her tomorrow and let her know the church is fine.*

As he climbed into bed Christy asked, "What were the scriptures about?"

He replied, "Oh nothing. Sister Snyder is just worried about us changing with the times."

Christy said, "Well she sounded really serious. Almost prophetic."

He replied, "I'll call her tomorrow and relieve her fears. I'm beat. This bed feels so good. I may just sleep all day tomorrow. Goodnight."

"Goodnight." Christy echoed.

At exactly 3:23 a.m. the phone on Pastor Patrick's night stand came to life waking him from his peaceful slumber. He answered it, still half asleep, "Hello."

In a panic Deacon Joe shouted through the phone, "Pastor! You have to get down to the church!"

"What's wrong?" answered Pastor Patrick who was now waking quickly.

Deacon Joe replied, "It's the church. She's on fire!"

Chapter 4

Pastor Patrick's midnight blue SUV was racing almost as fast as his mind. How did his beloved church catch on fire? How bad was the damage? Was the fire out? His last question was quickly answered as he rounded the next corner. Absolutely not.

The fire was blazing and all of Lost Creek's fire department was fighting it. The giant flames roared from the windows and roof of Big Oak Christian Church in magnificent fashion. It didn't look as if the fire hoses spraying the flames were having any effect at all. He parked as close to the church as he possibly could. Police and firemen had set a perimeter blocking the public from getting too close to the danger. After a few minutes of taking in the disaster and realizing the church was going to be a total loss, he approached one of the policemen.

"Excuse me, officer. I'm the pastor of the church here."

The policeman replied, "Yes, Pastor Patrick! I recognize you. I was in the service this morning."

The service this morning. The words filled his mind like a thick fog. Was it really only a few hours ago when so many people were laughing and celebrating in this very building? This beautiful building that was now an inferno.

He came back to the moment, "Is there anything I can do?"

"Not really right now, Pastor. Just keep your distance. This is the most incredible fire I've ever seen!" answered the eager young policeman.

The pastor thanked him and moved toward a small group of people who had gathered watching the blaze. Everyone's eyes were fixed on the massive building engulfed in flames. One man broke his gaze away from the raging fire.

"Pastor!" exclaimed Deacon Joe. He broke his mesmerized stare away from the fire to his good friend. "Joe. What on earth happened? Do they have any idea how this might have started?"

"No, it's too early to know anything according to the fire chief. You know him, Jordan Bates. I talked to him a little while ago. The fire has only been going about twenty minutes, but it spread quickly. Probably a total loss, Pastor," said a disheartened Deacon Joe.

8

Pastor Patrick knew in his head he needed to build up those around him. He should give them hope in the midst of the storm. But all he could do was helplessly watch his beautiful church burn to the ground.

Several hours later, Deacon Joe and Pastor Patrick slowly walked through the black charred rubble of their beloved church. They had been there all night watching the fire destroy the building they loved so much. There was nothing to salvage from the ashes. The pastor now stood in approximately the same place where, just hours ago he had announced how successful his church had been. He envisioned the high oak ceilings, the purple cushioned pews, the majestic stained glass window behind the luxurious baptistery, and the golden chandeliers that lit the sanctuary so brilliantly. All of it, now just a memory.

Deacon Joe broke the silence, "This is the work of the Devil himself, Pastor! But I think we should use it as an opportunity."

The pastor really wasn't focusing on what was being said. For some reason he wasn't able to focus on anything. It was as if he was walking in a daze.

He replied, "What do you mean, Joe?"

"Well Pastor, we can build her bigger! We had grown out of this building anyway. Let's build a church to hold a thousand people!" Deacon Joe exclaimed.

He hadn't really thought about the future yet. But, as usual, he liked what Deacon Joe had to say. "That's not a bad idea, Joe."

As the two men stood in the black debris they were interrupted by a ladies voice from the parking lot, "Pastor Patrick."

He looked up to see Caroline Stewart, the church's insurance agent.

"Hey, Caroline, We'll be right there," he replied as they began to make their way toward her through the destruction.

Caroline spoke first, "Pastor Patrick. Joe. I'm so sorry for your loss."

"Well, it's a tragedy, but fortunately no one was hurt. We will be okay," said the pastor slowly.

"Yeah. Satan got this round, but we're gonna come back stronger than ever." added Deacon Joe.

"I heard about the fire on the morning news. I immediately opened your policy to review your coverage." said Caroline.

"Thank you so much." replied Pastor Patrick.

"Don't thank me too quickly. I have good news and bad news." Caroline said.

Deacon Joe interrupted, "What do you mean?"

"Well, Joe, the church is fully covered and we will cut you a check today for a part of your claim, so you won't have to wait very long to have some capital to provide services for your congregation," said Caroline.

"Well, that's good news," replied Pastor Patrick. He had broken a sweat and for some reason everything seemed to be slowly spinning around him. He tried to ignore it. He was attempting to focus on Caroline, but it was becoming difficult.

She continued, "If you remember, when I came and met with the Church Council and the Deacon Board you voted to opt for a lower rate coverage. The plan you chose gives you the cash amount of your depreciated existing structures, but not the replacement costs at today's prices. Put simply, you're entitled to the price you paid for the building minus the depreciated value. That won't be enough to build the church back the way it was at today's prices. And if the bank calls your mortgage, which can happen in a catastrophe like this, then you will have to pay them off before you rebuild. Of course, you can turn around and get another loan if that happens."

Pastor Patrick remembered the meeting. They had agreed to the cheaper coverage because the church was in so much debt. They were spending almost their entire budget on facilities and staff. It seemed wasteful, at the time, to spend more on insurance than was absolutely necessary. Things like helping the needy and mission work weren't a very high priority either.

"Why is everything spinning?" thought Pastor Patrick. "I feel so sleepy. Are those black spots real?"

"Pastor! Are you ok?" exclaimed Deacon Joe.

He could hear their voices, but the black spots kept getting larger. It felt so peaceful.

Deacon Joe shouted, "Someone call an ambulance!" as Pastor Patrick collapsed.

Chapter 5

"I think he's coming around!" Patrick heard a familiar female voice say.

"Patrick, can you hear me?" asked an unfamiliar male voice.

Pastor Patrick was so comfortable, but felt like he was coming out of a deep sleep. He was confused as to where he was and why he was sleeping so well.

He opened his eyes and saw his wife Christy standing over him on one side and a man in a white lab coat and glasses on the other side. Sunshine was pouring into the room through a window. The man wearing the white lab coat said, "Just relax, Patrick. Do you know where you are?"

"I have no idea." answered a groggy Patrick Spakes.

"Honey, you gave us quite a scare," said Christy in a very anxious but relieved tone.

He asked, "What happened?"

"Patrick, I'm Dr. Davis, a neurologist. You passed out at the church."

The church. Oh yeah. For a moment he had totally forgotten about the tragedy.

Dr. Davis continued, "I believe you're fine. We were worried you had suffered a cerebrovascular accident - a stroke. But your CT scan and MRI were negative. Looks like you overdid it and your body needed a break. I believe with some good rest and fluids you will be back to normal in no time."

He replied, "That's great. I'm sorry."

"You don't have anything to be sorry for, Sweetheart!" insisted Christy. "You just rest and get better."

He closed his eyes and was back to sleep immediately.

When he woke up again the room was dark. He could hear the beeping noise of some kind of monitor. He looked over to his right and saw Christy asleep in a chair beside his bed.

Pastor Patrick spoke up, "Christy…Christy."

She stirred a bit and then realized he was awake and calling for her.

"Sweetheart! How do you feel?" asked Christy.

"I'm okay. How long have you been up here?" asked the now clear headed but curious pastor.

"You collapsed this morning. It's Monday night, or I guess Tuesday morning now. So I've been here about eighteen hours." answered Christy sleepily.

He responded, "Honey, I'm so sorry."

Christy interrupted, "Stop saying you're sorry. You have worked harder than anyone should. Patrick, when they called and told me your condition, I realized how much I really love you. I really want our marriage to succeed. I'm going to do all I can to be the best wife I can be for you."

Patrick was quiet for several minutes grasping Christy's hand.

Then he said, "Christy, it sounds as if you haven't been happy with our marriage. Are you happy with me?"

Christy teared up and said, "Patrick, I love you with all my heart. You get so focused on your career you forget how much I need you. How much the kids need a daddy who is there for them. I know you don't realize it, but you give your best to others and we get what's left over. Which isn't much these days."

He took a deep breath. He wasn't angry or defensive. She was absolutely right. He hadn't been able to see it until right now. He looked into Christy's beautiful eyes and said, "You are the greatest gift God has given to me aside from my Salvation. You and the kids are the most important people in my life. I promise I will show you how much you mean to me from now on. I always say the most important things to me are God, you, and the kids in that order. I will start living that way."

Christy collapsed onto her husband's chest and they held each other tight. She raised up and gave her husband a kiss. Something was different in that kiss. It was a wonderful feeling of a rekindled love and a fresh start.

Christy sat up beside his hospital bed and smiled. Then she remembered, "Oh, I brought your Bible."

She reached out and flipped on an overhead light. He looked at the bedside table. He reached over and picked up his black leather bound Bible. Like a flash his mind raced back to the last time he had held this book. He had nonchalantly looked up one of the passages Sister Snyder had prophetically given him. He shivered at the thought of that encounter. How she had warned him of God's coming judgment and how he had ignored her. He opened his Bible to the scrap of paper where he had jotted down the scriptures she had given him. He hadn't even looked at the second verse, but he would do that immediately.

Christy excused herself to go speak to the nurses and update any church members who might still be in the waiting room.

He thought to himself, *Okay, Sister Snyder, let's see what else God has been telling you. I underestimated your relationship with Him didn't I? Well, that won't happen again. Okay, here it is,* Exodus 23:19: "You shall bring the choice first fruits of your soil into the house of the Lord your God. You are not to boil a young goat in the milk of its mother."

"*I tithe!*" thought Pastor Patrick. *I always give ten percent of what I make. And I'm not planning on cooking any goats! This doesn't make any sense. I need to talk to Sister Snyder.*

At exactly seven a.m. He called Sister Snyder's home. He had waited three and a half hours stewing over what this verse was supposed to mean to him. But he didn't want to wake up a ninety-two year old woman too early.

On the third ring she answered, "Hello."

"Sister Snyder," he exclaimed eagerly.

"Brother Spakes!" I've been up most of the night praying for you. I'm so glad to hear your voice. How are you feeling?" asked Sister Snyder with genuine concern.

"I'm feeling better. The doctor says I'll be fine. Thank you for asking. I'm sorry to be so direct, but I looked at the verses you gave me Sunday. Do you remember?"

After pausing for a moment Sister Snyder answered, "Yes, Brother Spakes."

He exclaimed, "The second one doesn't make any sense. I tithe ten percent and have since I've been in ministry."

There was silence on the phone for a long time.

Finally Sister Snyder broke the silence, "I am not the one you need to be talking to Brother Spakes. God will reveal to you what you need to learn from that passage. But have no doubt, that is the scripture God has laid before you. He will reveal what you need to know if you seek His wisdom."

He was quiet as he gathered his thoughts. He then said, "Sister Snyder, I have taken you for granted the entire time I've been the pastor here. You are a good and godly woman. You are both wise and kind, and I'm sorry I haven't been the pastor I should have been for you. Please forgive me. And thank you for your prayers. Please keep praying for me."

With tears filling her eyes Sister Snyder replied, "I forgive you as my Savior Jesus has forgiven me."

Pastor Patrick said goodbye, hung up the receiver, and wept.

Chapter 6

It had been one week since the great church fire and the resulting health scare of their pastor. On this Monday afternoon he was reflecting on the previous week's events. He had experienced the goodness of God's grace and mercy in incredible ways. A spiritual revival had taken place in him, and he felt as close to God right now as he ever had in his life. He had been released from the hospital the past Wednesday morning.

He had cancelled all church activities and services for the upcoming week, against the wishes of Deacon Joe. Then he turned off his cell phone and spent the entire Thursday evening with Christy and the kids. It was wonderful. He spent the next three days praying during the day and being with his family at night. During this time, God revealed to him once again how much He loved him.

He was amazed at how far his career in the church had taken him away from his first love of worshipping God. He remembered when he was first saved how much he wanted to give his all to the Lord. He couldn't remember the last time he had felt the Holy Spirit this intimately, but it was refreshing to experience the love of God so powerfully again.

The Lost Creek Fire Department confirmed the fire was an accident started by faulty wiring. They asked Pastor Patrick to cancel any activities on the church grounds for the coming week due to dangerous clean up equipment around the church property.

He told Big Oak Christian Church members to visit church with relatives, have a family worship time, or to go be a blessing to another church in Lost Creek on Sunday. This had really irritated Deacon Joe and some of the other deacons. They discussed it at length while they played golf that Sunday morning.

For his part, Pastor Patrick led his family in a devotional and then took them hiking and enjoyed the beautiful day. They all really enjoyed the time together. After the hike they ate a picnic lunch Christy had packed.

After reflecting on the week's events he felt God wanted him to focus on the second scripture Sister Snyder had given him. He opened his Bible once again to Exodus 23:19. He had meditated on this verse a lot the past few days. God revealed to him he needed to build his church's stewardship foundation on the principle of giving God their first fruits. He would spend the next week putting the truth of God into a plan of action. This would be

15

a huge change of direction for the church, but he knew this was where God was leading them.

Pastor Patrick lined up the Lost Creek High School auditorium to have services in for the next few weeks. It would hold five hundred people, which should be sufficient. The only other option would have been to hold services in the multipurpose building adjacent to the burned rubble of the sanctuary. It would only hold about three hundred people, and currently there was a lot of construction equipment in the area excavating the burned structure.

He knew the message God was leading him to share would challenge many of his members' faith. He felt guilty that as their pastor he hadn't built a deeper faith in them. He had never truly challenged them to trust in God and to really be led by the Holy Spirit.

As he worked on the finishing touches of his sermon he called Christy to his study. "Hey, Baby, could you come in here and let me ask you something?"

Christy loved the new way her husband was including her in his life and their decisions. She also liked him spending quality time with her and the kids, and how he affectionately called her names like "Baby" and "Sweetheart" again.

"Hey! How's the sermon coming along, Handsome?" Christy answered as she entered the study.

"I was just finishing up and I wanted to talk to you about it. You know this is really going to challenge our church, and I'm worried they aren't ready for it. Do you still think it's what I should share?" he asked.

This was something new to the Spakes' relationship. Not since their first year of marriage had Patrick asked Christy for her opinion of what he was preaching. She felt honored to have some input into this area of her husband's life again.

"Well, we've prayed about it, and I believe God has really made it obvious this is where He wants you to lead. I believe you need to put your trust in God and do what you know He wants you to do." answered Christy.

"Thank you. It is the right thing to do. I just wanted to make sure we are in agreement, because this could be tough. Let's pray God will show up in a big way tomorrow, and allow our congregation to hear and understand His will," he said.

He took his wife's hand and they knelt to pray for God to be in control of their family, their church, and their future.

Chapter 7

Big Oak Christian Church couldn't have asked for a nicer Sunday morning to begin their services at the Lost Creek High School auditorium. The sun was bright and warm. The air was cool and crisp. It was one of those perfect spring days you dream about.

Today marked another new step the Spakes were implementing. They were all riding to church together in one car. Pastor Patrick felt like this would be a good way for them to spend more time together. Christy loved the idea. Daniel and Jamie went along with it, although it didn't seem like a big deal to either one of them at first. That changed when their Dad told them to put their cell phones away and then began asking their opinions on current events. What really blew their minds was when he actually listened to what they had to say.

As they pulled into the high school parking lot, he noticed kids playing outside and some of the youth ministry students huddled together talking and laughing. It looked like there was going to be a big turnout for the first "off campus" service.

Love Auditorium was built about two years ago for the school orchestra and theater classes. It was a great makeshift chapel. The deacons and planning committee had done a wonderful job transforming the auditorium into a suitable place for worship. In front of the podium was a small banner with the church's name and logo. There was an American flag behind the right side of the podium. Ficus trees lined the back of the stage creating a warm welcoming feeling in the room. Pastor Patrick made sure there were chairs lined up in front of the stage, facing the crowd, creating an altar.

He went and joined a group of men. They took turns shaking his hand and welcoming him back, or in one case jokingly accusing him of taking a golf vacation.

"Well, well. Decided to come back to work I see." he heard his good friend say.

"I'll tell you what, a guy misses one week at church and the deacons fall apart." He replied turning to grasp Deacon Joe's hand.

"Fall apart? We've been running smoother this week than we have in the past four years!" quipped Deacon Joe.

"Yeah, I might need to start worrying," laughed Pastor Patrick. "You might realize you don't need me! This place looks great! Good job guys."

One of the deacons asked, "So what's the plan, Pastor?

Deacon Joe added, "Yeah, I'd like to know the plan of attack myself."

"The plan right now is for me to get on that stage and welcome these folks. You know we are having church this morning!" said Pastor Patrick enthusiastically as he excused himself from the group.

He headed for the sound booth to pick up his cordless mic and get a quick lesson on how it worked. As he made his way to the front of the auditorium he saw Sister Snyder sitting down. He went immediately over to her.

"Sister Snyder! Good morning!"

She replied, "Good morning, Brother Spakes!"

"It's great to see you here. Sister, I will be very anxious to hear what you think about today's sermon." He said.

"Well, now I'm excited to hear what you have to share with us." she replied.

"It's not so much what I have to say as it is what God wants to reveal to us. I really need you to pray for our church this morning." He explained in a serious tone.

"I like the sound of that! Of course I'll be praying." answered Sister Snyder.

"Thanks! Now I better get things going or people are going to wonder if they have a missing pastor again!" He said as he hurried to the sound booth and then up onto the stage.

"Welcome, Big Oak Christian Church, to your home away from home! I am here to tell you God doesn't reside in a building. He lives inside of His people! Big Oak isn't gone. Big Oak is here together this morning to worship the King of Kings and Lord of Lords! Let's worship Him now in song!" proclaimed Pastor Patrick.

The worship leader, Alvin Bond, began the music and the praise was great. Everyone seemed to be enjoying the new facilities and set-up.

Deacon Joe noticed Pastor Patrick raising his hands during worship, which was a little unusual for him. After four songs there was a pause for prayer and time to take up the offering. As the instruments continued to play Pastor Patrick stood up and called the ushers forward.

Normally he would ask one of the ushers to pray, but this morning he took it upon himself to pray for the offering about to be given. No one was expecting the passion of the prayer about to be made.

"Dear gracious Father God, forgive us for putting so many idols before you in our lives. Please take this dirty, filthy, worldly money we're about to give and use it for Kingdom work. Please forgive us for stealing from you to finance our selfish pleasures. Thank you for your grace and mercy, but most of all thank you for the cross. Amen."

This prayer from his heart moved everyone in the room.

The Holy Spirit was stirring the hearts of the people. Most of them had never heard such a passionate prayer. It wasn't only the powerful words, but the love and conviction they were feeling. All of them were now curious to hear their pastor share what was on his heart. Sister Snyder's heart leapt at the obvious movement of the Holy Spirit, while Deacon Joe sat wondering what had gotten into his good friend.

After the offering was taken, Sky Burleson and Chloe moved forward to perform. He played the guitar and she sang, "The Wonderful Cross". It was the most powerful song they had ever performed together. Many people were moved to tears, and others just sat in awe. God was in this place. When they finished they got a standing ovation and several "Amens."

Pastor Patrick took the stage and stood in silence looking over the crowd for what seemed like an eternity. Normally he would open his message with a joke or funny story. Not today. As he finished silently looking at every face in the crowd he said, "I stand before you today, a sinner saved by grace. I have something to ask from each of you here today. I need to ask for your...forgiveness."

The auditorium was so quiet you could have heard a pin drop.

He continued, "I have been your pastor for almost four years. I have not challenged you or taught you to trust in God. Oh, you might be thinking, Pastor you have grown Big Oak every year since you arrived. That is true, but only in numbers. I really don't believe I have developed you spiritually. Have I led you to a place where you acknowledge your sin and repent of it? Have I taught you to be selfless and give everything you have to God? Do we corporately pursue holiness and righteousness? Do we pray for ways to help the needy and then act on those prayers? I'm not saying we need to be more religious. I'm saying we need to be completely God's.

One area God has recently convicted me to repent of, and let me tell you, this is one of many, is how I give my money to the church. Oh, I've given ten percent of my gross income since I went into ministry, but I was giving out of obligation. I looked at giving my tithe just like I looked at paying any

20

other bill. God calls us to be generous with our possessions. Everything we have is from God and we shouldn't limit our view of what is God's to ten percent of our check. What you give to the church should be a sacrifice you cheerfully give to God. It shouldn't only be our money, but our very lives. I haven't been giving cheerfully or sacrificially. The Lord has opened up my eyes to the beauty of His Bride, the Church, and has shown me how wonderful and joyful it is to give to her."

Deacon Joe thought to himself, *Pastor, you had me worried there for a minute. This is actually a great angle. Now reel them in and announce how we're going to build a larger state-of-the-art church building!*

Pastor Patrick continued, "There is another bride God has been convicting me about. My bride, Christy. This beautiful woman the Lord graciously gave me to care for. Honestly, I haven't done a very good job of that at all. But grace is a wonderful thing. Christy and I have rekindled a love that I, quite frankly, had forgotten existed. She shared with me she had all but given up on us ever really being happy together again. If you are struggling in your marriage, I am here to tell you there is hope. I had an addiction. Not to pornography or drugs. But an addiction just the same. My addiction was to worldly success. I wanted to have the largest church and be seen as a great preacher. I wasn't working to please my Savior. I was working to feed my pride. Working to be a winner in the eyes of men, not the eyes of God. I have been humbled by God, and I have begun to put my priorities in the correct order.

How can you know where your priorities are? It's simple. Look at where you spend your time, your talents, and your treasures. We will be talking more about this tonight at the multipurpose building on our church campus. I know we don't traditionally meet on Sunday nights, but I'm asking anyone who wants to be challenged spiritually to meet there tonight at six o'clock."

By this point Deacon Joe was furious. What was Pastor Patrick thinking? He should be casting the vision of building a new cutting edge sanctuary. Instead he's talking about fanatical spirituality, having a bad marriage, and giving up Sunday nights.

On the other side of the church literally and figuratively, sat Sister Snyder praising God. Just over three years ago, she didn't understand why God was leading her to support Patrick Spakes to be the pastor of Big Oak Christian Church. She didn't see the spiritual maturity and leadership she knew Big Oak needed. She fasted and prayed for fresh guidance, but kept feeling God was calling this man to lead her church. She couldn't go against what the Holy Spirit was telling her. So she gave Brother Spakes, as she chose to call him instead of Pastor, her blessing and support. The small remnant remaining in her church, especially Deacon Joe, was glad to have her blessing in pursuing Patrick Spakes.

She reflected on these events as tears of joy rolled down her face. A few aisles up tears were flowing from another lady's eyes.

Christy Spakes was so proud of her husband. The obvious changes he was making to obey God and love her and the kids was wonderful. She knew this morning's message would be tough on the congregation. But she felt the Holy Spirit moving and hoped the people would respond.

He finished up his sermon with a bold challenge. "Church, The Lord is good and gracious. He loves you just the way you are, but He loves you too much to leave you that way. He desires for you to change and become more like Christ. I will preach whatever the Holy Spirit leads me to share. I challenge you to search your hearts and see what God wants you to repent of and give everything to Him."

During the invitation several people came forward. Many of them were convicted of sin and in tears. But many others sat there in conviction, uncomfortable, but unwilling to repent. Most of these people were wondering what happened to their laid back preacher who never used to talk about sin.

Chapter 8

That evening Pastor Patrick and Christy entered the Big Oak Christian Church multipurpose building hand in hand. The morning service had been exhausting both emotionally and spiritually. After a great lunch, Daniel and his dad shot some hoops. Christy and Jamie went for a bike ride.

Deacon Joe had approached his pastor after the morning service, but was told they would have to talk about any details concerning the church after the Sunday evening service. Pastor Patrick wasn't about to miss time with his family arguing over decisions about the church.

Over the past two weeks he had communicated all the short term plans concerning the church with Deacon Joe. This was necessary to keep the church moving through all the chaos. Deacon Joe would always use the opportunity to try to persuade Pastor Patrick on the long-term direction of the church and planning the new sanctuary. He explained to him early on that he was prayerfully waiting on God's direction for Big Oak, but Deacon Joe was not happy about having to wait.

Pastor Patrick realized proverbial lines in the sand would be drawn over his new leadership style. Big Oak would lose some members who enjoyed the social aspects of the church, but wouldn't want to be challenged to totally submit to God and even sacrifice for him. It was with prayer and fasting he had discerned this path and he would follow God no matter the cost. As Christy got to her seat he stood before his people.

"It is exciting to see all of you here!" proclaimed an energized Pastor Patrick.

There were about eighty people in attendance. The pastor was filled with joy as he surveyed the audience. He wasn't worried about the number of people there whatsoever. He was happy to see Sister Snyder sitting with Christy and the kids. JJ was sitting with them too. Chloe and Sky were near the front sitting hand in hand. Deacon Joe was sitting near the back with some of the other deacons and their finely dressed wives.

He continued, "I appreciate you navigating the cleanup equipment outside and sacrificing your Sunday evening to be here tonight. I know this is a unique time in the life of our church. Tonight we're going to forgo worship in song and spend some time in prayer. Then I'll be sharing what I believe the Lord wants us, as a congregation, to do."

With that he offered a heartfelt powerful prayer for God to allow the Holy Spirit to lead them and open their hearts to follow God's will. After praying, he began his message.

"God is in control of everything. Nothing happens outside of His power. He allows good and bad. Through all situations He loves us. He gives and He takes. We don't always understand why He does what He does, but He expects...no He commands us to worship Him at all times and in all circumstances."

He paused for a moment. He knew his next words would be tough for many of his members to hear. After a short breath of prayer for strength, he continued.

"The gospel is the core of everything we are in Christ. Salvation is found only by God's grace and we cannot add anything to it by our works. As we abide in Christ He will lead us. As we follow Him, our actions will reflect Christ in us.

God has laid out biblical principles for the individual Christian and for His Church to follow. He has given us time on this earth. He could have taken us straight to Heaven the instant we were saved. But He chose to leave us here for a purpose. This precious time is to be used for Him. God has also given us talents. He gives each believer a Spiritual gift or gifts that He expects us to use for Him. You may not think you're very talented, but God can use you in some incredible ways. God says even giving a cup of water to someone who is thirsty can make an impact for His Kingdom. God has also given us treasures. We live in one of the richest countries the world has ever known. We are commanded by our SAVIOR...our GOD...the One we say we trust our eternity with to have nothing before Him. All our stuff, our things, our money are His. He expects us to use these treasures to invest in His Kingdom. The only treasures we will really be able to keep are the ones we store in heaven."

His voice was now booming and powerful. At this point the Holy Spirit was moving throughout the people.

He continued, "As your pastor I have done a poor job of teaching you these truths from the Bible. I have not lived out these principles for you to see. Once you are saved by His amazing grace, God has a ministry for you. It isn't always being a missionary or a preacher. But every Christian is a minister. And God has a ministry that is made just for you. He wants you to use your time, talents, and treasures for His Kingdom. These three t's,

24

bathed in prayer with the foundation of the gospel, are what God uses to reach the lost people in this world. I don't believe God wants us to have a building fund drive, or even think about building a new church sanctuary until we submit in this area of stewardship. These three t's are what I believe God wants to use to build this church."

He continued speaking slowly and intentionally, "I would like for each of you to consider taking a one year challenge. Over the next year, will you completely give God your time, talents, and treasures? Don't enter into this lightly without a lot of prayer. I would recommend you even fast before taking this challenge. If we really accept this, it will most likely cause us to sacrifice a lot. However, I believe it will also allow God to grow and bless us in some incredible ways.

If you decide to accept this challenge, spend some time asking God to reveal how you can use these three t's for Him. I would like Big Oak to grow spiritually, physically, and financially according to our faithfulness in this. If God wants to use us, I pray we will give Him our best.

I am accepting this 3t Challenge. I don't say this flippantly or without counting the cost. If I'm not totally submitting to God's leadership and leading you to grow closer to Him, I will resign as pastor of Big Oak."

An audible gasp came from the congregation. The weight of this moment was clear.

He then said, "Next Sunday night I want to meet again at this time and get some feedback from you. You are the Church! A fancy building cannot replace you or your impact in the world for the Kingdom of God. So this week please pray and consider how The Lord wants you to use your time, talents, and treasures for Him."

With that and a powerful short prayer, he dismissed the astonished congregation.

Hector Gonzales was smiling from ear to ear as he approached Patrick Spakes standing at the back of the Big Oak multipurpose center. Most of the members had filed by the pastor on their way out. Christy and the kids drove Sister Snyder home. Some people gathered in small groups to discuss the evening's challenge and the dramatic changes taking place with their pastor. Most people were affected by the message and weren't too chatty. Hector was an exception. He grabbed Pastor Patrick's hand and exclaimed, "Great message, Pastor!"

Hector was an adamant supporter of Patrick Spakes. They had met in unusual circumstances neither man would ever forget.

Two years ago Hector's wife, Elizabeth, was in the hospital with complications from the delivery of their son, Pedro. Pastor Patrick was there to visit an elderly member of Big Oak when he first heard, and then saw Hector in the surgical waiting room sobbing uncontrollably. He hesitated to approach Hector, but in a rare moment of yielding to the Holy Spirit he approached the hurting man. It took him a while to get Hector's attention between sobs. He introduced himself and explained he was a minister. Hector regained enough of his composure to tell him about his wife's critical condition. Elizabeth was in surgery and the doctors were giving her a very slim chance of surviving. He assured Hector the doctors were very good and that God was concerned about his situation. Hector didn't really believe in God, but allowed the pastor to pray for him and his wife.

The following day, Patrick had to go to the hospital again to visit another church member and ran into Hector. Elizabeth had survived the surgery and was responding well. Over the next week he went to the hospital to visit Hector, and eventually Elizabeth and Pedro.

Elizabeth miraculously healed up quickly and went home healthy.

The Gonzales's lived on the other side of the capital city in a much lower income area known as Westside. Even so, they traveled every Sunday to Lost Creek to attend what Hector called "Pastor Patrick's church."

Most people in the Big Oak congregation accepted the Gonzales family, although some questioned the Biblical correctness of their marriage since he was Hispanic and she was Caucasian. Hector was the only minority in Big Oak Christian Church.

Given the serious mood of the evening, he was happy to see Hector.

"Thank you so much Hector. I really appreciate you coming this evening. I know it's a long way home for you." He said.

"It's no problem, Pastor. I wouldn't have missed tonight for anything." replied Hector.

"You really challenged us this evening. We have a lot to pray about and consider." added Elizabeth who was holding their sleeping two year old son.

"Well you two have a lot to offer. You are such a wonderful encouraging family. How's Pedro these days?" asked Pastor Patrick.

"He's growing like crazy. And is ready to play soccer!" exclaimed Hector.

26

"Slow down there, Papa," interrupted Elizabeth, adding, "He tripped over the soccer ball trying to kick it. I don't think that means he's ready to play!"

They all laughed.

"Well I would love to talk all night, but I know you have a long drive home. Be safe."

The Gonzales's left after sharing hugs with their pastor.

As happy as seeing Hector and Elizabeth made Patrick, he knew his next encounter would be the toughest he had ever faced.

Chapter 9

Speaking with the Gonzales family filled Pastor Patrick with joy. The feeling quickly faded as he turned around to see Deacon Joe locked on him with an ice cold stare. The two men walked intentionally toward one another. This was the moment Pastor Patrick had been praying about for the past two weeks. His emotions were mixed with great hope and awful dread.

Deacon Joe had personally pushed for Patrick Spakes to become the pastor of Big Oak Christian Church four years ago. The two men clicked immediately. They were soon playing golf weekly and watching their sons play ball together. Both of them approached growing a church like growing a corporation. This business just happened to have God as the product. When searching for a pastor, Deacon Joe was successful in winning support for Patrick from the few members remaining after the scandal. He was elated, and more than a little surprised, when Sister Snyder not only went along with his recommendation to hire Patrick, but threw her support completely behind him. The two men were a natural fit. As the church grew so did their friendship.

Pastor Patrick spoke first, "I'm glad you're here, Joe. We need to talk."

He responded angrily, "Yeah Patrick, I think it's about time we spoke."

He mentally noted that was the first time since being hired Deacon Joe had not referred to him as "Pastor."

"Joe, I've been going through a lot. God has really been dealing with me. I'm sorry I haven't been able to spend much time with you, but I have really needed to step away and refocus on the Lord." He said.

Deacon Joe replied, "That doesn't make any sense. We have always talked about God together. Why all of a sudden can't we discuss things?"

He said, "No we really haven't, Joe. We haven't sought after God together. We have made plans and asked Him to bless them. We have taught classes and formed programs in God's name. We have raised money in the name of Jesus to fund our ideas of what church should be. But we haven't ever really humbled ourselves before Almighty God and asked for His will to be done in us and in our church. We haven't honestly asked Him to allow us to succeed where He wants us to succeed and fail where He wants us to fail."

Deacon Joe exclaimed, "So is that what you want for our church? Failure? That might explain why you've cancelled services and even encouraged members to visit other churches!"

Remaining calm he replied, "No, Joe. Absolutely not. Our church building burned down and we didn't have time to organize a service. You know that. That's why I told our members to take the Sunday to spend with their family or attend another Christian church. But more important than that is how we measure success. We measure it in such a different way than God does. Take Jeremiah for instance. By the world's standards he was a failure. God called him to specifically preach to people who wouldn't listen. Isaiah was the same way. And so were many of the prophets. The world saw them as failures, but in God's eyes they were incredible success stories!"

Deacon Joe replied flatly, "So now you're saying if our church is vibrant and growing then we're a failure. And if we're empty and not doing anything we're a great success? Well you should love your burned down church then."

Pastor Patrick said, "Joe, you know that's not what I'm saying. And God's church didn't burn down. God's church met in this building tonight. God's church has withstood burning, beatings, and torture. God's church, Joe, is His people. We have been trying so hard to get people into our fancy building so they can be more like us. That's something we've been really good at doing. But God wants us to be the church inside and outside of a building. And He doesn't want people to be more like us, but more like Jesus."

Deacon Joe responded, "You're beginning to sound like a fanatic."

He replied, "A fanatic? Really? Because I want to live out the principles of the Bible? Because I want to spend time with my wife and kids? Because I want to literally live out the commands Christ gave us to follow? You know what, Joe, we have played golf once or twice a week for the past four years, and I've never invited a sinner to play with us. I've invited prospective church members, but never because I was worried about their eternal home. Just their church home. It's not the same thing."

Deacon Joe replied, "Patrick, you have gone through a scare. I'm giving you all the space you need to get ahold of yourself. But as head deacon of this church, I will not allow you to go off the deep end with these fanatical ideas. At least not as far as the church is concerned."

He began to answer, but paused. Then he said, "Joe, you are right. You are a leader and a protector of this church. I will listen to your words and pray fervently for God's direction. But, Joe, I have to tell you this: I have to do whatever God calls me to do, even if you disagree with me and even if it strains our friendship."

Deacon Joe replied, "Well, Patrick, I guess the ball is in your court now. I want things to go back to the way they were before, and not let Satan have a victory in this mess."

He looked at Deacon Joe, right into the black of his eyes and said, "Joe, our friendship is very important to me. I really want us to grow in Godliness together and overcome these differences. I've been praying and fasting for God to open your eyes the way He's opened mine. I know that probably upsets you to hear, but I want you to experience God's love the way I have the past few weeks."

Deacon Joe replied, "I'll see you later, Patrick." Then he turned away and walked out the door into the darkness.

Chapter 10

The next week was full of surprises. Pastor Patrick met with Sister Snyder for some good council. He was amazed at how godly of a woman she was, and how much wisdom he was gaining from spending time with her.

On Tuesday he met with his staff individually and then corporately. He encouraged them to share what God was doing in their lives and what their vision for their ministries were. He also encouraged them to spend time with their families. They sensed the phenomenal change in him and were excited about the vision he was beginning to share with them.

For their size, Big Oak Christian Church had a comparatively small staff. Pastor Patrick was obviously the lead pastor. Alvin Bond was the worship minister, Clint O'Dell led the youth and children, and Judy was the church secretary. Pastor Patrick hired ambitious people and expected the most out of them professionally. The deacons took up a lot of the responsibilities of the church. Deacon Joe had an efficient group of men. Pastor Patrick and Deacon Joe realized early on that Big Oak couldn't afford a large staff, so they put big expectations on the ones they had. They did, however, pay their staff very well; especially their pastor.

Pastor Patrick recognized God was leading him to change the whole philosophy of ministry at Big Oak and he wanted his staff to be prepared. Change is never easy in a church. He encouraged them to seek God's wisdom. He was sorry he hadn't been a better mentor spiritually for them. Earlier he had asked for and received their forgiveness. No more time was going to be wasted worrying about the past. It was time to move forward. He warned them that God was calling him to preach some hard things and to prayerfully prepare to minister to those who would struggle to apply these principles.

Wednesday night he visited the youth service and was impressed by Clint's message. Clint related how practical the 3t Challenge was for teenagers. Pastor Patrick knew that in every great awakening the youth have played a major part in it. At the end of the service, Clint announced they would be forming a youth worship band. Since Daniel played the guitar and Jamie sang, he wondered if they might volunteer.

On Friday Alvin Bond, the worship leader, stepped into Pastor Patrick's office and asked to speak with him.

"Sure. Come on in, Alvin." He answered.

"Pastor, I just got a call. My home church where Missy and I are from offered me the worship leader position. With Missy pregnant we could be there with both of our families when our baby is born. That's always been our dream and it seems to be falling miraculously into place." said Alvin hesitantly.

He replied, "That's great, Alvin. It sounds like this is an answer to prayer. Of course I hate to see you leave Big Oak, but I know you have really wanted to be near your family. Have you discussed this with Missy?"

Alvin said, "Yes, I called her immediately. We really feel like God wants us leading worship there. We agreed to continue to pray about it, but unless God puts up a huge stop sign we're probably going to take it. I'm sorry."

He stepped around his desk, put his hand on Alvin's shoulder, and said, "Don't ever be sorry for following God and putting your family's welfare in line with His plan."

Alvin replied, "I'm afraid people will feel like I'm abandoning ship. Things are tough right now with the church building burned down and all."

"Alvin, God is in control and Big Oak will be exactly what He wants it to be. You have been a shining light here for three years. I wish I would have been a better mentor for you, but the best advice I can give you is to pray fervently, love your family, and trust God."

Alvin turned and hugged Pastor Patrick with tears in his eyes. He stepped back and said, "Thank you so much. I was worried you would be upset. I love Big Oak and all of the people here. I honestly believe there is something special about to happen here. I hate to miss it, but I'm happy to be going home."

He said, "I'm happy for you, Alvin. I hope God blesses your family and ministry abundantly. We will miss you and Missy."

Alvin replied, "Thank you, Pastor."

Pastor Patrick smiled and Alvin left. He pulled his office door closed and knelt down. He said in a whisper, "Lord, what are you up to now?" Then he spent a long time in prayer.

Saturday the Spakes family went to Daniel's baseball game. He was the starting third baseman as a junior. He was also working on his pitching, hoping to be in the starting rotation his senior season. JJ, Deacon Joe's son, played second base. JJ's parents weren't at today's game for some reason. Lost Creek won 4-2, and Daniel had two hits in three at-bats. But the proudest his parents were that day was when Daniel led the guys in the

32

Lord's Prayer after the game. They went out to eat on the way home and had a great time. After getting home and some prayer time as a family, they got ready for bed. As Pastor Patrick drifted off to sleep, he thought about the past week and the changes that were coming to Big Oak. He knew tomorrow would be another tough service for a lot of the members.

Chapter 11

Sunday morning the Spakes family enjoyed a delicious breakfast and rode to Love Auditorium together again. The crowd was slightly smaller than the previous week. Pastor Patrick wondered to himself if it was because of the challenge he made to truly follow Jesus. After speaking with several members, He took the stage. He opened with announcements and had the entire assembly laughing and enjoying themselves.

Even Deacon Joe was laughing and thinking to himself, *this is the Patrick Spakes I know! Maybe our little talk opened his eyes.*

They transitioned to worship in song and it was even more powerful than the week before. God the Father was exalted. God the Son was praised. God the Holy Spirit was moving. People could feel the presence of the Lord. When the Holy Spirit comes into the presence of unholiness, sin is revealed and decisions are made. People choose to either submit to God or harden their hearts. These decisions were being made all over Love Auditorium this morning. Many wept and begged God for forgiveness, while just as many shut down and lingered in their guilt.

Pastor Patrick stood up to pray after the worship set was done. Behind him on the screen popped up the words "1st Trinity United Church." Pastor Patrick asked everyone to look up at the screen. Now, if Big Oak Christian Church had a rival it would be 1st Trinity United. As everyone looked up at the screen, He said, "Today we begin a new chapter in our fellowship. Each week we will be choosing another church and we will pray for them."

A somewhat confused feeling swept across the auditorium.

He continued, "Now, I know some of the questions you have about this: Why would we start praying for other churches when our building is burned down? Why don't we focus on praying just for our church right now? What happens if God blesses these other churches at our expense? Well I have been guilty, as many of you are, of seeing other Bible believing Christian churches as our competition. That's not Biblical and it is sin! We worship the Lord Jesus Christ and His Bride is the Church, not Big Oak Christian Church. Now Big Oak makes up part of the Church, but it's not just us. Its 1st Trinity United and 1st Baptist and Sardis Missionary and Landmark Methodist and 1st Pentecostal and all churches that teach truth as revealed in scripture. We don't all agree on everything. But if a church anywhere teaches the fundamental beliefs of Christianity, then we should support and pray for them.

If a church believes in the authority of the Word of God then we have common ground. Then, if they teach one God revealed in Father, Son, and Holy Spirit, and Salvation found in the grace of God through faith in the death, burial, and resurrection of Jesus, we can have fellowship with them.

Do NOT confuse my words here. We must be careful not to accept any and all beliefs if they aren't Biblical. But it seems we view other Christian churches as more of an adversary than the Devil. Satan and Sin are our enemies! Not other Believers!"

He then led his church in a prayer that included asking God to bless his once viewed rival 1st Trinity United Church.

After prayer he launched into a passionate sermon based on the Good Samaritan. He challenged the church to follow the previous week's message on giving God their time, talents, and treasures. He explained and offered the one year 3t Challenge to the Sunday morning assembly. He stressed he didn't want to become legalistic about it, but that Big Oak would be basing all her ministries on these principles.

After singing a hymn of praise, he announced Brother Alvin had something to share.

Alvin stepped to the mic and said, "Big Oak has been home to Missy and me for three great years. This past week we have been offered the opportunity to lead worship in the church where we grew up and were married. Both of our families are there. We have accepted this offer and in two weeks we will be moving. I want to thank all of you for being such a great church, and for all the wonderful memories and friendships we have made here. I honestly believe Big Oak Christian Church has a fantastic future ahead of her. Finally, I want to especially thank Pastor Patrick for giving us the privilege of serving here. Thank you."

The church was in shock.

Pastor Patrick said some words of appreciation for Alvin and Missy, then reminded the congregation there would be a six o'clock meeting in the multipurpose building. With a short prayer he dismissed the service.

Deacon Joe was seething and questioning everything about his church's pastor. He knew it was time to act.

35

Chapter 12

At exactly six o'clock that Sunday evening there were two very different gatherings of Big Oak Christian Church members taking place.

Deacon Joe had invited eight of the fifteen members of Big Oak's deacon board to his home. He had called them for a special meeting to discuss the direction of the church. Of course he only invited those who he knew would agree with him and follow his lead.

Deacon Joe began, "Gentlemen, we are at a pivotal point in our church's history. Many of you weren't here just a few years ago when we were on the brink of collapse. I helped lead us away from that cliff and I'm telling you we're headed down another dangerous path. As you all know Patrick is one of my closest friends."

Most of the men noticed he used Patrick's name. They had never heard Deacon Joe refer to him as anything other than "Pastor".

He continued, "My church comes before my friends! I'm afraid the trauma from the church fire and subsequent health scare has given him over to a bit of fanaticism. I hate to say it, but he doesn't seem like the same man to me. As deacons, it is our responsibility to protect our church from radicalism."

The men nodded in agreement as Deacon Joe continued to form his treasonous plot.

Meanwhile, across town Pastor Patrick was speaking to around one hundred members in the multipurpose building.

He said, "As you can see the clean-up is about complete. I'm prayerfully planning our short term and long term goals. Tonight is not about buildings and programs though. Tonight I want to open the mic up for you to share what God is doing in your life. Many of you have called and texted me stories this week, so I want to give you the opportunity to share your stories with our whole church family. First, we're going to have some worship in song."

Chloe and Sky led the gathering in two praise songs and the Holy Spirit quickly moved throughout the congregation. After the music was finished Pastor Patrick invited anyone who wanted to share their testimony to come forward. There was a microphone up front and person after person went forward to share what God was doing in their lives. Many shared they had finally received God's free gift of Salvation. Others said they had already been saved, but had never followed through with the command of Jesus to be baptized and wanted to do that now. One man shared how he had quit smoking and was now giving that money to the church. A woman shared how she had been a closet alcoholic for many years. She went to her first AA meeting after Pastor Patrick's challenge. She said it was like being freed from chains when she obeyed God. A couple stood up together and said they had been on the verge of filing for divorce, but decided to give their marriage another chance. They had been to their first counseling session on Friday. Confession after confession filled the church with love.

Daniel stood up next. "Many of you have assumed for years that I am a Christian. I'm a preacher's kid, so how could I not be? I would have told you last month that I was a Christian. I prayed a prayer when I was young, but honestly a month ago there was no difference in the way I lived and the way the world lives. The events with my dad and our church have opened my eyes to the truth. If I am a Believer, then I will be a follower. Jesus said, 'Follow me' over and over. Following is an action. It's what we do, not just what we say. I have a long way to go to be the person God wants me to be, but I want all of you to know that I am a real Christian now. A follower of Jesus."

Pastor Patrick stepped up and hugged his son. Then he said, "Well, I guess we're going to need to have a baptism service for all our new brothers and sisters in Christ!"

He encouraged them a bit more and then closed the service.

Afterward Hector Gonzales came up to Pastor Patrick, "What a night, Pastor! God is really doing something special here."

"Yes He is Hector. How are you and your family doing?" asked Pastor Patrick.

"We are good. We have accepted the 3t Challenge and are excited about it. But I have a favor to ask you." answered Hector.

"What can I do?" He asked.

"My cousin, Victor, is a preacher in Westside where we live. He is a good man, but he is overwhelmed. Our city is not like Lost Creek. There are many poor people, crime is a problem, and I feel Victor needs some encouragement." said Hector.

He thought for a moment. Then he said, "I'll tell you what, give me directions to Victor's and I'll drive over Thursday. I have the day off. But only if you let me take your family out to dinner Thursday night!"

Hector laughed and said, "Just come to my house. I'll take the day off from work. Good luck getting Elizabeth not to cook for you!"

The men laughed and said their goodbyes.

At the same time Pastor Patrick was showing the last few members out of the church, Deacon Joe was dismissing the remaining men from his home.

Two plots were forming. A storm was brewing. The future of Big Oak Christian Church would rest on the outcome of the coming showdown.

Chapter 13

Pastor Patrick was well rested Thursday morning and excited about going on his trip to visit Hector in Westside. He ate breakfast with his family and headed out. He decided to take the route around the capital city since traffic would be brutal at this hour. He also enjoyed the natural landscape much more than driving through the big city.

As he drove, he thought about his Tuesday morning meeting with Sister Snyder. After he had shared with her about this visit, she had told him to be sensitive to the Holy Spirit. She felt God was telling her to pray especially hard for him. He also thought about his phone call with Deacon Joe. Pastor Patrick had called him, as he did weekly, to confirm everything for the upcoming week's activities. Pastor Patrick told him he had missed him Sunday night. Deacon Joe had replied that he was busy doing the Lord's work. When he inquired to what that meant, Deacon Joe changed the subject and then ended the call. He was wondering what Deacon Joe was up to as he pulled his SUV into the Gonzales' driveway at nine-thirty. It had taken forty five minutes to get there.

Hector Gonzales popped out of the front door as he was walking up the driveway.

"Pastor! It's good to see you my friend." said Hector enthusiastically.

As he grasped Hector's hand he said, "Good to see you too. Do you realize the last time I was here you had just brought Pedro home?"

"I know, Pastor. It has been too long." said Hector.

The two men went inside and shared some coffee. After catching up, the conversation turned to Hector's cousin, Victor.

"So tell me what's going on with Victor." He inquired.

Hector answered, "He is a very good man. A minister like you. He loves helping people. He does a lot for this community. But he has gotten frustrated lately. Our town has a lot of drug use, prostitution, robberies, domestic abuse, just a lot of crime. Many people who used to help him have stopped, and he has less and less money because of the hard times and bad economy. I think he is frustrated because he is working so hard, but he doesn't have much help."

Pastor Patrick looked at Hector and said, "It sounds like he could use some encouragement. Hector let me ask you something. Why do you drive

39

all the way to Lost Creek every week to attend church when you have a cousin who is a preacher right here in Westside?"

"You led me to the Lord, Pastor. You have helped me grow in my walk with Him. I love listening to your sermons each week. I help Victor out when I can around here. We used to go here on Sunday nights before Big Oak started having the Sunday night gatherings. I love learning from you!" said Hector.

He smiled and said, "I love you being a member of Big Oak. Our story is a great one. But Hector, God is a lot bigger than me. If He ever wants you somewhere else, you have to be willing to obey him. God's will is more important than what we want. A lot more important!"

Hector answered, "You've got a deal. I wouldn't want to disobey God to follow you. But you will always be my Pastor, even if I move to the North Pole." Both men laughed.

He said, "Why don't we head over to Victor's and see what we can do to encourage him." Then he added, "Hector, what are you doing off today?"

Hector answered, "I took a vacation day from the shop. I told them my pastor was coming to visit. I always tell them what a good man you are."

Pastor Patrick was humbled. He thought to himself, *Not nearly as good a man as you are, Hector. Not nearly as good.*

As they drove to Victor's church, he looked at the town and the people in a new way. They didn't just look like masses of poor people with different skin tones. They looked like people who needed to hear of God's love and have someone share that love with them. Pastor Patrick was so much more sensitive to the Holy Spirit than he had been just a few weeks ago.

Hector was pointing out landmarks and important places as they drove through the city. They passed the school and kept going. They continued about a mile and pulled up to a rundown old building that looked like it should be condemned. Over the door was a beat up old sign that read "Westside Hope Center".

Pastor Patrick thought to himself, *really?*

Hector led him through the creaking front door of the rundown building. It smelled old and musty inside. They walked across a room that Pastor Patrick figured was the sanctuary for services and the large group area for afterschool kids. They entered a hall with several small rooms on either side.

Hector called out, "Victor! We're here, Bro."

From a room at the end of the hall came a reply, "In my office. Come on back."

As they entered Victor's cramped office he stood up and greeted the men.

"Hector! It is good to see you. And you must be Hector's infamous pastor. It is good to finally meet you." Victor shook their hands and asked them to have a seat.

There were two chairs sitting in front of Victor's wooden desk. Other than the laptop on his desk everything looked very old and worn out. A bookcase held several worn-out books, some pictures, and a couple of trophies. On the walls were some more pictures, a dusty American flag, and some "Live Drug Free" posters.

The men talked for a while about their families and got to know each other. Finally Pastor Patrick asked, "Victor, you are obviously a good man who loves and serves others. Why am I here?"

Victor looked at him and took in a deep breath. Then he said, "When Hector mentioned you coming by earlier this week, I wasn't happy about it. I was offended that he had asked some preacher from Lost Creek to come 'fix' all of my problems here in Westside. Then I stopped and asked myself why I was so upset. I realized I am at my wit's end. We have had so many setbacks lately with the economy and there are so many hurting people, I think I am losing hope. I don't understand why God is allowing so much pain."

Pastor Patrick allowed Victor's words to sink into his spirit. He didn't want to give some trite answer to a man who had just opened up his heart to him. Victor had some legitimate needs and concerns.

He looked the young pastor in the eyes and said, "Victor, I'm not here to 'fix' everything. I do feel like God led me here for a reason. I would like to learn more about you and your ministry. I would love to hear what God is doing around here."

Victor laughed under his breath and said, "What God is doing? Well, I'm not sure I can answer that. I still believe in God, but He hasn't been doing much around here lately. I'm helping kids after school that don't have enough to eat. I'm taking care of single moms who are raising kids in horrible situations. I'm trying to do more with less, and I don't know how much longer I can do this."

He said, "Victor, it sounds like you are doing a lot. In fact, it sounds like you are doing too much. I was in your shoes not too long ago. I discovered I wasn't giving God enough room to work. When I came to the end of myself, God took over. Jesus was telling the truth when He said that our burden is light when we follow him. Victor, do you remember when you first experienced God's grace?"

Victor replied, "Yes. I remember when I was saved."

"Yes, but I would like for you to really think about that experience. Take a minute, close your eyes, and think about the feeling of God calling you. Where were you? What was your life like back then? What were you doing?" asked Pastor Patrick.

Victor closed his eyes and began thinking back to that night. He was a soccer player at Westside High and attended a Fellowship of Christian Athletes rally at a local church. He actually went to see a girl he was attracted to who was involved with FCA. A football player from a nearby town who had made it to the pros was speaking. He talked about how God's love wasn't conditional, but was based upon His grace. He shared John 3:16 which says God so loved the world that He sent His Son so that anyone who believes in Him will have everlasting life. Then the football player asked if anyone wanted to become a follower of God. Victor didn't totally understand what he was doing, but he knew he wanted to learn more about Jesus. He went forward to speak with a volunteer. They explained how everyone has sinned. Victor knew that already. He had made a lot of bad decisions in life. The volunteer then told him that God required people to be sinless to enter Heaven to be with Him. Since men chose sin the only perfect substitute would be for God's Son, Jesus, to become a man and sacrifice His perfect life for all people. Since Jesus had done this incredible thing all men could once again be with God, if they put their faith in His Son. Victor completely believed in Jesus and discovered his purpose in life by doing the work of God. Jesus' love overwhelmed Victor that night. The same love was overwhelming him once again this morning. Victor began to weep and slipped out of his chair to his knees thanking God for His love. They spent a long time in refreshing prayer.

Chapter 14

As the men finished their prayer time, Pastor Patrick said, "Victor, why don't you show me around the Hope Center."

Victor smiled and replied, "I'll be happy to give you the grand tour."

The three men walked out of Victor's cramped office, down the hallway back toward the front entrance.

"These rooms are used for Sunday school classes and after school tutoring rooms. We have one young man, Dwayne, who uses a room to teach guitar lessons. Up ahead is the main room. It's where we have service on Sunday mornings and large group events after school. It will hold about eighty people. We only average about fifty people on Sundays." explained Victor.

Pastor Patrick asked, "How many kids are active in the after school program?"

"About fifty to seventy students depending on the time of year. It's a longer walk than I would like from the school. I try to walk with them when I can. When it gets warm outside a lot of the older kids will skip to hang out at other places. That's usually not the best scenario for young unsupervised teens. Drug use, alcohol abuse, and teen pregnancies increase in our kids during that time. The peer pressure and lack of supervision is just too much for most kids to handle. I really feel like if we had more to offer the older kids it would help. I would also like to have more volunteers and more volunteer training for them. You have helped me realize I have been trying to do too much and I need to delegate more responsibilities around here." said Victor.

"Your facilities look like they are a little worn out. Is that something you're concerned about?" He asked.

Victor answered, "Oh, most definitely! The kids have to wear their coats inside in the winter and it won't cool off in the summer. The poor energy efficiency of this building cost us two or three times more than it should to heat and cool. To add insult to injury, I just got a call from the management company that our rent is going up! I'm really not sure how we're going to make it."

Hector added, "Yes, Pastor, and what's really sad is a man at our church owns this property. His name is Ty Stephenson."

He repeated his good friend's name, "Ty? He owns this building?"

43

Victor answered, "He is the owner and has a management company who operates it. We pay our rent to them. But they won't fix anything or help get any upgrades. They basically ignore me, unless I am late with our rent. Which, praise the Lord, hasn't been often."

He said, "I apologize on behalf of my friend Ty, but this may be an answer to our prayers. He's a good man and if he knows your need then maybe we can work something out. Ty is one of my golfing buddies and a member of our Deacon Board. God may just be orchestrating something special. Now, Victor, what about outside? Do you use anything outdoors?"

The three men walked to a side door. There were a few swings and an old see-saw in a dusty space that had seen better days.

Victor said, "Obviously we don't have much, but the kids play out here on pretty days. There's no fence to protect the kids. We have to watch out for shady characters who come by sometimes. We have to be careful. They aren't a problem if an adult is around."

Pastor Patrick replied, "Yes, I guess that's something you have to be aware of."

His mind was busy processing all of the dangers these innocent kids have to face growing up here. It was breaking his heart. He knew God wanted him to act, but He wasn't sure how to move forward. He had gained enough wisdom over the past few weeks to know not to rush into anything like the old Patrick Spakes would have done: See a problem, fix a problem; no need to bother praying to God about it.

He said, "Victor, I'm not sure what God wants me to do here, but I feel He wants me and my family and, quite possibly, Big Oak Christian Church to be involved. I would like to partner with you to pray over our churches and their futures."

Victor replied, "Sounds great to me."

He then turned to his other friend and said, "Hector, we are going to have to talk about your future soon my friend."

Hector answered, "Okay, Pastor. But first I think it's time to grab a delicious lunch from Lola's!"

They all laughed and headed for the front door.

Chapter 15

Lola's Taco Shack was a Westside favorite. The men decided to take
Pastor Patrick's SUV. Victor said if they left such a luxurious car there they
may never see it again.

As the men drove through downtown Westside, Pastor Patrick got
another up close look at what life was like in the poverty stricken
neighborhood. There were rundown buildings, people begging at the corners
and several groups of young men just walking the streets without any
obvious purpose. He would have been very judgmental toward these people
a few weeks ago, but today his heart was breaking for them. They seemed to
him as sheep without a shepherd. No purpose. No hope. Just existing in life
without a real reason for living.

"Up here on the right," instructed Hector.

He pulled into a parking space at Lola's Taco Shack. The place was
packed.

"Hope you're hungry, Pastor, because this is gonna be a treat! Lost Creek
has some good restaurants, but Lola's tacos have soul!" exclaimed Hector.

He replied, "Great, because I'm starving. Oh and guys, lunch is on me. So
eat up!"

"No way, Pastor. You're our guest," said Victor as the men piled out of
the SUV.

As the three men walked into the restaurant people immediately began
speaking to Hector and Victor from all around. They hugged and shook
hands with people as they made their way to the counter. Pastor Patrick felt
stares that said, "What are you doing in Westside?"

One particularly large rough looking guy with a neck tattoo of a pair of
dice stepped in front of him and asked aloud, "Who's your preppy friend,
Victor?"

Many of the other patrons stopped to listen to Victor's reply.

Victor smiled and speaking up for all to hear said, "This is Pastor Patrick
Spakes. He is a minister of God and my friend. This is Patrick's first time to
Lola's. He is in for a treat isn't he, my friends!"

Everyone laughed and the large tattooed man stuck out his hand, smiled,
and said, "Any amigo of Victor's is an amigo of mine." To the relief of
Pastor Patrick.

After a delicious meal and lots of talking with the other patrons, the men took a tour of Westside.

Victor and Hector showed him all around. They avoided some particularly rough spots, but he got to see the majority of the town. There was one park in particular that caught his eye. People were obviously dealing drugs and there were some prostitutes roaming around, but he felt especially led to pray for Redemption Park.

At about two-thirty Victor said, "We better get back to the Hope Center. The kids will be getting out of school soon and I need to be there."

Once they were back to the center, Victor was surprised he wanted to stay and see the after school program in action. It was an early spring day outside so they were preparing some indoor and outdoor games. Hector was getting some snacks ready. Victor and Pastor Patrick walked down to the school to escort some of the younger kids to the Hope Center.

He noticed again how far the center was from the school. Today it wouldn't be an issue with the nice weather, but on cold or rainy days it would be a long walk for kids.

The school bell rang and almost immediately kids came stampeding toward the waiting men. Victor introduced Pastor Patrick to them and they were happy to tell him all about themselves. One little girl took his hand and he carried her backpack for her. She asked him questions all the way back to the Hope Center. It reminded him of how Jamie used to talk and talk when she was a little girl. The kids bounded into the Hope Center like it was their home.

Hector had plenty of desserts and lemonade ready for them. The kids loved talking to their new friend, "Pastor P". He and Hector entertained some of the kids, while Victor checked on a group of older kids and two women volunteers in the tutoring rooms.

Pastor Patrick noticed one teen who was tuning up his guitar for a lesson. He immediately thought of Daniel. He told the young African American, Dwayne, that his son played the guitar also. They talked until one of the younger kids interrupted saying he and his friends wanted to go outside and play. He found Victor and asked if it was okay.

Victor said sure. He grabbed a soccer ball and turned to leave, but then he stopped and asked Victor, "What do I do if a drug dealer comes up?"

Victor laughed and replied, "Well don't buy the kids any drugs. It's not like an ice cream truck in Lost Creek! Seriously, you don't do anything. Let Hector deal with them or come get me. I'm pretty sure you'll be fine."

So he headed out to play. The kids broke up into two teams with Pastor Patrick and Hector as the team captains. This reminded him of when Daniel would have several friends over and they would play basketball or football in the backyard. He wished Daniel was here now. He would love playing with these kids.

At six o'clock Victor was closing everything down and getting the remaining kids packed up and out the door. The three men headed over to Hector's. He was asking Hector where his family would like to go out to eat as they entered his home.

Hector smiled as he opened the door and said, "How about Elizabeth's Diner?"

As the men entered the house, the delicious smell of spaghetti and meatballs filled the air.

"Hector! I told you I would take you out to eat tonight." He exclaimed.

A jovial Hector replied, "And I told you, good luck getting Elizabeth not to cook for you. Honey, you have upset the pastor!"

Elizabeth entered the living room wearing an apron and said with a big grin on her face, "I hope my spaghetti and homemade meatballs will help make him happy again."

He laughed and said, "If they taste as good as they smell, I'm sure I will be very happy!"

Victor's wife Maria joined them a short time later.

After a great meal and some talk about the day's events, Pastor Patrick excused himself to head home. Hector and Elizabeth gave him big hugs. Little Pedro gave him a hug also. He and Victor agreed to meet by phone and pursue God's plan together.

Pastor Patrick was cruising on the two lane road home around the capital city. He was thinking about the experiences of the busy day: meeting his new friend Victor, eating at Lola's, and spending time playing with the precious kids. What would God want him to do to help out here? How could Big Oak invest in changing lives in another community? He was thinking about how Ty should be able to help, when out of nowhere a deer sprang into the road!

He hit the brakes and swerved. Fortunately the deer didn't stop and he avoided colliding with him. Whitetail deer were plentiful in this area and hitting one could damage or even total your car; not to mention what could happen if you swerved off the road. Pastor Patrick's heart was racing. He thanked God for protecting him and slowly accelerated toward home, much more aware of his surroundings.

Chapter 16

Daniel called out to his dad, "You coming old man?"

Pastor Patrick yelled back, "Alright, now it's on! Get ready to eat my dust!"

The guys decided to spend this beautiful Saturday morning cycling the river trail. The route they chose to ride today was about ten miles long. Pastor Patrick was in good shape for his age, but there was no way he could keep up with an athletic multi-sport seventeen year old.

With his dad's challenge still in the air, Daniel raised up off the seat and pumped the pedals with all of his might. He took off like a rocket. His dad just smiled and kept peddling. He turned a corner about a mile up the trail and saw Daniel. He was sitting by the river with his bike parked beside him. Pastor Patrick pulled up and stopped.

"What's wrong? Run outta steam?" asked his dad jokingly.

"I was afraid I might have to call an ambulance if I didn't make you stop and take a break." answered Daniel.

He smiled and said, "Don't worry about me. I'm just pacing myself. Life is a marathon, not a sprint young man."

Daniel just smiled and looked out across the beautiful river gently flowing downstream. They sat there quietly drinking some water and catching their breath.

Daniel broke the silence. "Dad, can I ask you something?"

"Of course, Daniel. What's up?" answered his dad.

"You know how you've been teaching on the three t's. Do you really think our decisions should be based on God leading us in those areas?" asked Daniel.

He looked at Daniel and said, "There's a lot more in the Bible than just our stewardship for God, but I absolutely believe we should be obedient to following the Lord in those areas. God gives us freedom to follow Him or not. By giving Him our time, talents, and treasures we become less selfish and are able to be used by God. What's on your mind, Daniel?"

Daniel paused and then said, "I've really been thinking about giving up the travel baseball team. It takes up so much of my time, and I really feel like God has other plans for me this summer. I've really been experiencing some great things lately and I want to share God's love with others. I still want to play baseball next year for the school and I'll definitely stay in shape. I ran it past JJ and he said I was crazy. He said coach is going to flip out. What do you think, Dad?"

He gathered his thoughts then answered, "I think we should pray about this decision as a family, but Daniel this is your life, and if you feel led to give up summer ball I will totally support you. JJ is right, your coach won't be happy about this, but obeying God sometimes does require sacrifice. I know how much you love playing ball. I'm proud of you for being willing to give up something you love to follow Jesus."

Daniel said, "Thanks, Dad. There's something else. Can you tell me how you knew you were being called to ministry? I mean how did you actually know that's what God wanted you to do with your life?"

He was taken by surprise. He had preached and taught on how to listen to God more times than he could count. He had spoken with young men and women about pursuing ministry. Daniel had never shown any interest in becoming a minister whatsoever, so he hadn't considered Daniel following in his steps. He was filled with excitement.

"Daniel, I was sitting in a church service when I was 19 and I felt God speak, not out loud, but to my heart. I knew He wanted me to spend my life telling others about Him."

Daniel looked at his dad and said, "I can't say for sure I've gotten the call. I just want to be open to anything. I really want to serve Him however I can. Maybe through sports or music. I just don't know."

He said, "Son, you don't have to figure out your whole life today. God has a plan for you. Just follow Him day by day, and things will work out exactly the way He wants."

Daniel looked at his dad and said, "Thanks for listening, Dad. Do you think you've recovered enough to finish this trail?"

Pastor Patrick leaped up onto his bike and shouted, "Last one to the car buys lunch!"

Chapter 17

Sunday morning at 6:23 the Spakes woke up to a sound all preachers hate to hear: rain.

In the past it would have upset Pastor Patrick a lot. Not anymore. Christy rolled over and asked sleepily, "Honey, do you hear the rain?"

She was expecting an aggravated answer, but instead heard her husband yawn and say, "Aren't we lucky to have a roof that doesn't leak."

She giggled, and rolled over and snuggled up to him.

She said, "I'm sorry it's raining. I know attendance will be down because of it."

He replied, "Everyone that God wants to be there will be."

Christy smiled and said, "I love you."

Normally her husband would be angry and upset about bad weather on a Sunday. She knew it wasn't laziness or lack of caring that gave him peace this morning. He had contacted and encouraged people all week. She knew he was learning to do what he was supposed to do and trusting God with the rest.

Christy gave him a kiss on the cheek and said, "How about some breakfast, Handsome?"

He answered, "Sounds great."

He took a hot shower and then called Victor for a quick word of prayer. After getting the kids up, he went to the kitchen to help Christy with breakfast.

On the rainy drive to church, the Spakes family laughed and caught up on what they had done over the weekend.

Once they arrived at Love Auditorium, the attendance was about what was to be expected. Only about three hundred people. One interesting thing he noticed was almost all of the people who had attended the Sunday night gatherings were here.

He spoke to Hector and Elizabeth Gonzales, Sister Snyder and several other church members. He noticed Deacon Joe talking with a small group of men. He made his way over to them. He especially wanted to speak to one man in this group.

"Ty." Pastor Patrick said sticking his hand out.

Ty Stevenson shook the pastor's hand and said, "Good morning, Patrick."

51

Pastor Patrick shook the other men's hands and exchanged pleasantries.

Deacon Joe commented, "It looks like attendance is way down."

He replied, "Yeah, it's a shame that people are so fair weathered about coming to church. But it's good to see you made it."

He turned to his other golf buddy and continued, "Ty, I need to speak to you about something if you could hang around a few minutes after church today."

"I'm sure that can be arranged. I'll see you after church." answered Ty.

"Okay, gentlemen. Thank you for all of your hard work and commitment to the Lord. I really feel like major changes are coming." said Pastor Patrick.

Deacon Joe responded, "I think you might be onto something there, Patrick."

He looked at his old friend and sensed his ominous tone. He turned and headed for the stage. As he got closer to the front of the auditorium he felt a heaviness upon him that he hadn't felt in a long time. His walk slowed just before he got to the steps of the stage. He turned to his right, and kneeled down at the makeshift altar.

He quietly called out to God for help. He wasn't sure what was going on, but he sensed it was spiritual warfare. It was as if Satan himself was amongst this group of believers. As he was praying he heard Chloe begin to sing "Amazing Grace" acapella.

Then he began to hear others at the altar. He felt a hand on his shoulder. Sky Burleson was praying over him. After a few minutes of prayer a gentle peace fell over Pastor Patrick. As he arose he saw people up and down the altar crying out to God. He took the stage and praised God as Chloe continued to sing.

As the song ended he stepped to the microphone and said, "Isn't it good when God shows up at church?"

Some people initially laughed not realizing he was serious.

The rest of the service was good. During the invitation several members came to the altar again to pray. Pastor Patrick couldn't help but notice most of them were there last Sunday night. Those who had taken up the challenge of the 3t's. Giving their first fruits to God. He announced there would be a farewell for Pastor Alvin and Missy tonight following the gathering. He also announced that the next Sunday he would be presenting a vision for Big Oak Christian Church's future.

Deacon Joe glanced around at the other deacons sitting around him and smiled a smug grin.

After the service Pastor Patrick was shaking hands with people leaving Love Auditorium when he noticed Ty Stephenson standing over to the side. He excused himself and headed over to Ty.

"Thanks for staying after church, Ty." He said.

"Pretty lengthy service today with the extended altar call." answered Ty.

He smiled and said, "God was moving this morning. I prayed with someone to be saved and two others who want to be baptized! That's exciting stuff."

Ty smiled back and said, "So what is it you were wanting to discuss? You know if you would make it out to the golf course anymore we could discuss it on the links."

He said, "Yeah, Ty. I miss playing, especially with nice weather like we had yesterday. But I've been fasting some things that were coming between me and my relationship with God and my family. God has really been true to His word and blessed us."

Ty replied, "Really. How so?"

He said, "Well, to begin with, Christy and I haven't been this happy in years. Daniel is really growing spiritually, and Jamie seems much happier. Many people in our church have really come to know God in a deeper way. But I think it's more than Lost Creek that God wants to bless. Just this past Thursday I was able to visit Westside..."

Ty interrupted, "Westside? What the heck were you doing over in that ghetto?"

He continued, "Ty, I went to visit Hector Gonzales' cousin, Victor Martinez, who is a pastor there. He has a church and an outreach to underprivileged kids there called the Hope Center."

Ty looked deep in thought and said, "You know what? I believe I own the building that houses that church and mission center."

Pastor Patrick said, "That's what Hector and Victor told me. They also told me it hasn't been updated in years and the rent is about to go up. Possibly enough to shut it down."

Ty said, "Well the recession has held the rent down for a couple of years. My management team has told me it's time to go ahead and put some upward momentum on my investment properties."

53

Pastor Patrick replied, "Ty, the upward momentum is quite possibly going to sink this church. They haven't rebounded financially and are struggling to make ends meet. Kids really depend on the after school activities there to help them in a lot of ways. I realize you need to make a profit on your investments, but could you at least look into how much they pay and see if there's any way you can help them?"

Ty's voice carried a bit of anger as he answered, "Listen, I don't tell you how to run your church and I expect the same respect. I have a family to support and if my management team feels it is time to raise the rent, then I plan to raise it. If this church can't pay, then maybe God is done with them and has other plans. Whatever the case, I expect my preacher to stay out of my business affairs. And on a personal note, Patrick, I'm not sure of the direction you want to take Big Oak. I'm late for lunch. Is there anything else?"

He composed himself and his crushed expectations and said, "No, Ty. Thank you for hearing me out. Enjoy your lunch."

With that Ty Stephenson turned and walked out the door.

Pastor Patrick gathered his family and drove home in the rain. He was quiet and very disappointed.

Chapter 18

Big Oak Christian Church's multipurpose center had more people attending this Sunday evening gathering than ever before. About one hundred twenty people were there. Unlike the oppressed feeling of the morning service, there was very positive energy filling the room.

Pastor Patrick felt the energy as he entered the building. He really needed the boost after the conversation with Ty this morning. Although disappointed, he spent the afternoon praying and preparing the details of his vision for the church.

His spirit was quickened as he began to speak with his church members. Instead of small talk about the weather or sports, they were sharing stories of what God was doing in their lives.

After speaking with several people, he made his way to Sister Snyder who was seated already.

"Good evening, Brother Spakes." she said.

"Hello, Sister!" he replied. "How are you this evening?"

She answered, "I'm wonderful. But the Lord has put you on my heart all afternoon. Are you doing alright?"

He answered, "I'm doing fine now. God is breaking me of relying on myself. I thought I had an easy answer to a big problem, but it hasn't gone the way I had hoped. I was pretty depressed about it this afternoon. I'm realizing God must have another plan. I don't understand why it's not working out, but I am trusting God for an answer."

Sister Snyder said, "My Seth used to say, 'God always has a ram in the bushes'. He was talking about when Abraham was going to sacrifice Isaac, but God saved Isaac's life and sent a ram to sacrifice instead."

He replied, "Yes, I know the story well. It takes on a whole new meaning when God asks us to put our hopes on the altar."

Sister Snyder said, "It sounds like you're learning through this situation. Trust God and watch how He increases your faith through this trial."

"You always encourage and amaze me. Thank you, Sister. Okay, I gotta get this service started." He said as he headed to the stage.

He welcomed the congregation and led them in a word of prayer inviting God the Father, God the Son, and God the Holy Spirit to have freedom to move in their lives.

Brother Alvin led them in two songs of heartfelt worship. Pastor Patrick then took the stage.

He said, "Wow! Isn't it good to be in the presence of God with our brothers and sisters in Christ! Brother Alvin, you will be missed around Big Oak. We have a great going away celebration for you tonight following our gathering. But first I want to share some of what God has been showing me.

I'm so excited about the ideas and plans the Lord has been laying upon my heart. Tonight I want to share some of the vision I see for Big Oak.

Let me be clear, what I am sharing tonight is not an official budget request. We have a Deacon Board and Church Council that will lead our business meetings and help us navigate through the important decisions our church faces. Please be in prayer for these leaders as they seek God's direction."

He paused to look over his congregation and then continued, "God has been sharing a vision with me for our church. He has confirmed this through His Word and through what many of you have been sharing with me. Loving God and loving people will be our focus. Financially I see us being more generous than we have been in the past. I want to take the three percent we currently give to foreign missions and increase it to ten percent. I also want to give another ten percent away to domestic and local missions. That leaves us eighty percent for construction of a new church building, staff, and operating expenses. I was in Westside this past week visiting a friend of mine who is a pastor there. He is struggling in a tough area trying to share God's love with people who are hurting. He may even lose his building and an after school program that helps a lot of kids. I believe God would rather Big Oak invest some of our resources in people like this, instead of spending it on a new elaborate building. There are hurting people all around us, and I believe God wants us to help them."

Sister Snyder was basking in the vision Pastor Patrick was sharing.

He then said, "Don't misunderstand me here. If God leads us to replace our sanctuary we will. But we must do it in a way that honors Him. Not for our pride, but for His glory. We can build a nice building that is efficient for ministry without going into overwhelming debt. The 3t's fit perfectly into this vision. We will build our church programs around the time and talents you are willing to share. And we will base our budget on being generous with our treasures. There's a 20/80 principle in today's average American church. It says 20% of the people will do 80% of the work and will give 80%

of the money. I want Big Oak to do better than this. I believe you do as well. Just this past week I've spoken with several of you who have committed to increase your giving. Many of you are realizing God doesn't need our money, but He wants our hearts. It's a stretch for many of us, but your creativity is inspiring.

One retired couple is giving up a day each week to volunteer over at the nursing home. They are simply sharing their time loving other people.

Another man, who is a mechanic, is giving his talent to God. He has asked me to announce to the church that he is willing to work on needy people's vehicles free of charge one Saturday a month. I'm hoping to find some others who are interested in this ministry for him to mentor.

A single mom who is here this evening e-mailed me last Sunday night telling me she was increasing her giving. I received another message from her on Friday. She had gotten an unexpected raise. It more than covers the increase in her giving. Praise the Lord! Our God is faithful. There are lots of stories around here like these. Please be in prayer about how you can give God your 3t's over the next year. I know He is leading me to make some major changes in my life."

He closed the service with a word of prayer. He invited everyone to stay for the going away party for Alvin and Missy.

As everyone was rearranging the multipurpose center for Alvin's going away celebration, Buzz McCoy came up to Pastor Patrick.

"Excuse me, Pastor." said Buzz.

He answered, "Hey, Buzz. How are you tonight?"

Buzz, a middle aged accountant answered, "Pastor, I'm either losing my mind or God has spoken plainly to my heart. Either way, you're not going to believe what I'm about to tell you."

He looked at Buzz and asked, "So what is it you need to tell me, Buzz?"

"Pastor, I've been really burdened the past few weeks. I took the challenge you presented and asked God to show me how I could honor Him with my time, talents, and treasures. I've really been trying to be sensitive to Him. Until this afternoon I hadn't been led to adjust anything. But at four o'clock today that changed. I felt the Holy Spirit tell me to take one of my rental buildings and sacrifice it to God for one year. I didn't have any other guidance until you spoke tonight. While you were speaking about your friend in Westside, the Holy Spirit told me 'that's who you're supposed to help!'" explained Buzz.

Pastor Patrick couldn't believe what he was hearing.

He asked, "Buzz, where is this building located in Westside?"

Buzz answered, "It's about a block from the school. My renters just moved out so it's already vacant. Do you think he'll be interested?"

He exclaimed joyfully, "Yes, Buzz. I know he will be very interested!"

Buzz smiled and said, "Good! It's a great feeling to help other people. I want them to have it rent free for the next year. They can renovate the building however they want to fit their needs."

He grabbed Buzz and hugged him. Then said, "Buzz, you'll never know how your obedience has increased my faith. Thank you my brother. We'll need to discuss the details tomorrow. Can I come by your office?"

Buzz replied, "Sure, Pastor. Sounds good. Looks like they're ready for you to start the party for Brother Alvin. I'll see you tomorrow."

He said, "Okay, Buzz. Yeah, I better get up there. Thanks so much! God is so good!"

He swiftly moved back up to the microphone and observed, "Looks like everything's ready for our celebration tonight. Come on up here Brother Alvin and bring your lovely wife with you please. You ladies out did yourselves with the food in the back. Before we eat we have a few surprises for these two special people."

There were two chairs up front for them.

He waited for them to be seated and then said, "Let's bring the house lights down. Okay, go ahead with the video."

A video began to play up on the screen behind the stage. It had a picture of Alvin and Missy with the words "Thank You for Blessing Big Oak Christian Church" superimposed over them. Then a video began playing of people from Big Oak telling them "thanks" and wishing them well which played for about ten minutes. Once the video finished Pastor Patrick stepped back up to the mic. The house lights came up and he said, "Brother Alvin, would you like to share a few words?"

Alvin took the microphone and shared his gratitude for Big Oak and the people he had been able to minister to. Everyone gave him a standing ovation. Pastor Patrick asked him to lead the congregation in a final worship song. Alvin paused for only a moment and then led them in his favorite old hymn, "Victory in Jesus".

Afterwards Pastor Patrick said, "Brother Alvin, Big Oak has taken up a love offering for you and Missy. Here's a check to help you move and maybe buy some diapers for your little one."

Alvin replied, "Thank you so much for everything. We have taken the 3t Challenge and plan to share it with our new congregation. God is good and I'm glad He allowed us to be a part of Big Oak the past few years. You will always have a special place in our hearts."

Their pastor said, "Christians don't ever really say 'goodbye'. It's more like 'until we meet again'. So Brother Alvin and Missy, may God bless you and keep you until we meet again. Please head to the back and get something to eat. I'm sure everyone will allow your beautiful pregnant wife to eat her dessert before they all get their going away hugs."

Everyone laughed.

The evening had gone great. Pastor Patrick slipped outside and called Victor. He was overcome with joy and relief. God was answering their prayers and building their faith.

Chapter 19

Monday morning Pastor Patrick met with Buzz McCoy about the building. Buzz had four investment properties. Two of them were located in Westside. The one he was donating to the Hope Center had most recently housed a pizza restaurant. He got all the paperwork necessary for Victor to be able to move in. It would take about four days to finalize everything.

He met Christy for lunch then e-mailed all the Board of Deacons and Church Council members his budget requests for the upcoming year. He asked to have an official church business meeting the coming Sunday night to present the budget. The insurance company was going to be depositing the remaining amount of money from the fire. The church needed to have a plan moving forward.

Tuesday he met with Sister Snyder. He was always amazed at her faith and wisdom. She surprised him by asking him to be her power of attorney. She had already made out a will. He was honored she would trust him with such a personal task. They discussed her wishes in the event of a medical emergency and aspects of how she would like her funeral held.

Tuesday night he played basketball with Daniel and JJ. Wednesday he met with several church members throughout the day. He noticed the ones who had taken the 3t Challenge would share what God was doing in their lives or how they were applying the challenge. Others who hadn't taken the Challenge talked to him mostly about when a new church building would be built, or what they thought it should look like. He loved all of his members, but felt his spirit quicken when talking with those who were pursuing God. He prayed for the Holy Spirit to draw more people to worship God, instead of buildings and preachers.

Wednesday night he sat in with the youth and watched Daniel play the guitar in the new youth worship band. He did a great job and Clint really challenged the kids using the story of Jonah. Many responded to the altar call. Pastor Patrick loved seeing youth seeking God at an early age.

Thursday he spent the day with Victor in Westside looking over the new facility Buzz had donated. It was perfect. Only one block away from the school and plenty of room for services and tutoring. They would need to renovate and decorate it, but that wouldn't be too hard. The back of the building was large and already fenced in for security. There was plenty of room to play games out there and with a little attention they could have a great playground area.

Pastor Patrick headed home early that afternoon to catch Daniel's baseball game. Jamie had a recital that night. Her school choir had a performance in Love Auditorium. Saturday evening Pastor Patrick, Christy, and Jamie had just gotten home from the grocery store when Daniel burst into the kitchen.

He shouted, "Dad, you're not gonna believe this!"

Alarmed Pastor Patrick asked, "What is it, Son?"

Christy interjected, "Are you alright, Daniel?"

Daniel answered, "Yeah. I'm ok. But Dad's not!"

He said, "Slow down, Daniel. What's going on?"

Daniel said, "You've got to promise not to say anything to Deacon Joe about what JJ told me!"

He looked at Daniel and said, "I'm not promising anything. If there's something I need to know then you tell me. I will do my best not to mention anything you say to Deacon Joe, unless I feel it is absolutely necessary."

Jamie said, "Just tell us already."

Daniel looked at his dad and said, "Deacon Joe is planning on ambushing you at the business meeting tomorrow night. He's got enough of the Deacon Board voting with him to ask for a confidence vote from the church on you remaining in charge. He's been planning it all week. JJ doesn't agree with his dad about you, but he's scared to say anything. He thought you should know though. Dad, what are you gonna do?"

He stood silent for a minute and then said, "Well, first I'm going to finish helping your mom put away these groceries. Then I'm going to go review my sermon for tomorrow morning. God has this situation under control. Tell JJ not to worry. I don't see any reason to call Deacon Joe. But we all need to be praying for wisdom and courage. No one in this family is to say a word about this to anyone. Except to the Lord. We definitely need His help big time!"

Chapter 20

Sunday morning's service at Love Auditorium went great. The Holy Spirit had already providentially led Pastor Patrick to preach on God's sovereignty. As he taught on God being in total control, he felt like he was preaching as much to himself as he was to his congregation.

After lunch, he played some basketball with Daniel. Then he put the finishing touches on his budget request and his plan for handling Deacon Joe's confidence vote.

That evening he stood in front of his congregation and noticed there were a lot more people here for the business meeting than there had been for the previous week's gatherings.

The place was completely full.

Pastor Patrick took the stage and said, "It's so good to see so many here tonight for our gathering, which will be followed by the budget meeting. Sky and Chloe why don't you come on up and get us started with some worship. Following our worship in song, there will be an open mic for anyone who wants to share what God has been doing in your life."

Sky and Chloe opened with "Blessed Be the Name of the Lord" and then moved into more worship songs of praise. Afterward several people stood up and shared about how God was blessing their lives through the 3t Challenge.

Pastor Patrick took the microphone after about thirty minutes of testimonies and said, "I'm sorry to have to cut this off. I could listen to your wonderful stories of God's faithfulness all night. But we have to move on to our business meeting. We're going to have a ten minute break and then reassemble for the meeting."

After a word of prayer he dismissed the gathering.

Ten minutes later he took the stage again and announced, "I call tonight's business meeting to order. You should have a copy of the proposed budget for the rest of the year. As you can see, I'm recommending we increase our foreign missions giving from three to ten percent. I've also asked for ten percent to go toward domestic and local missions. With the remaining eighty percent I recommend we pay staff, bills and begin to look at a future new building for our church."

From the audience he heard a voice say, "Point of order speaker."

He looked over to see Deacon Joe standing up.

He answered him saying, "Deacon Joe. You are recognized."

Deacon Joe made his way to the front. He said, "The Board of Deacons have something to share with the church. May I have the floor?"

Pastor Patrick answered, "The floor is yours, Sir."

He took a seat as Deacon Joe began, "Before continuing talks on the budget, I have the unfortunate job of bringing a serious issue before the church. A month ago our church burned down and our preacher had a very serious health scare. Since that time, we have not had any real direction or discussions about building a new church. Attendance has also been going down. I have personally tried to discuss these issues with Patrick, but have only received vague answers. This is nothing personal. In fact, I wish this wasn't an issue at all. But, as the leader of the Board of Deacons, it is my responsibility to protect this church. The truth is, the majority of the deacons have very real concerns about our church and its leader. We have had difficult conversations and through these talks have come to the conclusion to recommend Big Oak Christian Church have a vote of confidence on Patrick Spakes remaining as our pastor."

The congregation sat in shocked silence.

Deacon Joe continued, "For those of you who don't know, a majority of the Board of Deacons or a unanimous vote of the Church Council can call for a vote of confidence on any staff member of our church. An eight to seven deacon vote brings the pastor's vote of confidence to the floor. All other business is tabled until after the vote. We will hold the vote of confidence next Saturday evening here in the multipurpose center. Absentee voting can be cast during normal business hours at the church office beginning tomorrow. We must not let personal feelings get in the way of what is best for our church. I think we can now close the meeting until Saturday. Thank you."

Pastor Patrick stood and said, "Point of order, Joe. I believe the by-laws state that when a staff member has a vote of confidence called, he has the right to address the congregation before voting begins. I would like to address my congregation now."

Deacon Joe was caught by surprise and stammered, "I guess it does say that. But you can address them Saturday if you choose."

He responded, "If voting begins tomorrow during business hours, I believe I will speak now."

Deacon Joe said, "Okay, Patrick. The floor is yours. We will be dismissed at the conclusion of your defense."

He smiled and took the mic. "This is not my defense. It is my vision. I am surprised the deacon vote was only eight to seven. Deacon Joe is usually better at manipulating people into following his way of thinking. I hold no grudge about these men calling for a vote of confidence. It is their duty to protect Big Oak from heresy or immoral leadership. Fortunately, I didn't hear any charges like those. What I heard was that these men don't like the fact we're not rushing into debt over building a new, fancy sanctuary. I believe a mismanaged building program was a big problem when I arrived here. They don't like the 'direction' of giving more away to the needy and keeping less for ourselves. If you agree with these men, that we should keep more of our money and do less for the needy, then please vote with them to remove me as your pastor. But if you feel that we should give our time, talents and treasures to serving others then vote for me to remain as your pastor. I feel I should share a couple of details about what God is calling me and my family to do. I'm going to ask Big Oak to decrease my salary by thirty percent. There's no way we can increase our churches giving if we don't cut our spending somewhere. I will also recommend we replace our full-time music minister position and salary to a part-time position with a smaller salary. Since we've begun the 3t Challenge our church donations have increased.

If you're wondering how we'll make it work in our home, here's our plan. We've already worked out a deal to trade our cars for older, but still dependable cars. Christy got a part time job at the school library. With some other cuts here and there we've been able to not only make our budget balance, but increase our giving to twenty percent. God is faithful!

I preached this morning on God being in total control. I fully believe that He is and always will be.

Finally, I want to close with this. I love Big Oak. I want to remain as your pastor because I honestly believe God wants me here. According to our church by-laws, I have to get fifty-one percent of the vote to remain as your pastor. But, I want you to know, if I don't receive seventy-five percent of the vote, I will take that as a sign I should resign. Please pray about how you should vote, but know that no matter how you vote, I still love you."

Chapter 21

The next week was filled with activity. Deacon Joe was actively soliciting people to vote against keeping their pastor. He spread gossip and half-truths to whomever would listen.

Pastor Patrick on the other hand was busy making plans for Big Oak's future, and helping Victor get some things organized for the "New Hope Center."

On Tuesday, He met with Sister Snyder. She shared stories of God's faithfulness when her husband Seth was in ministry. This gave him even more peace. He had learned that it wasn't up to him to keep his job. It was his responsibility to be obedient to God.

Saturday came quickly. He and Christy sat down with the kids to explain how the process was going to work. If the church vote was seventy-five percent or lower they would be stepping down as leaders of Big Oak. Anything above seventy-five percent and they would remain. Either way Pastor Patrick and Christy wanted their kids to know that they trusted God with providing for their family, and with the direction of their church. After a short prayer they were on their way.

The multipurpose center was overflowing with people once again.

The Spakes family entered the church and made their way to the front row where they had reserved seats held for them. Sister Snyder was sitting there waiting for them. He noticed Deacon Joe sitting on the other side of the church looking very smug.

He knew Deacon Joe had a lot of influence and that the vote might be very close. He didn't question raising the bar to seventy-five percent though. He had prayed about it and felt God wanted him to set the bar higher. If he couldn't trust God with that, then how could he hang on with fifty-one percent of the vote and ask people to put their trust in God?

Daryl Burchfield was the president of the Church Council. He would be presiding over the meeting tonight. The council was also in charge of counting the votes. He stepped to the mic and called the meeting to order.

"I would like to thank everyone for being here this evening. I call this meeting to order. I'm not happy about having to deal with this situation, but we have a check and balance system in place to keep power from being in very few hands. I respect our church by-laws and realize they are there for a reason."

Daryl continued, "At this point, the Head of the Board of Deacons who called for the vote of confidence, Joe Smith, and the staff member on whom it was called, Pastor Patrick Spakes, each have five minutes to address the assembly. Afterward, we will allow all eligible voters to cast their ballot for or against Patrick Spakes remaining the Pastor of Big Oak Christian Church. Deacon Joe, you have the floor."

Deacon Joe stood and approached the front. He cleared his throat and began, "Big Oak Christian Church, it was a tough decision to call for a vote of confidence on a man who you know was a very good friend of mine. I have tried and tried to remain patient about our direction as a church, but I haven't witnessed anything that leads me to believe we are getting back to normal again anytime soon. Patrick seems to be getting more fanatical as each day goes by. Our sons play ball together, we used to play golf regularly, and we worked many long hours together building this church over the past four years. I cherish those memories. But as I've shared with many of you this week, Patrick told me those efforts were a waste of time because we were succeeding where God may want us to fail. I don't understand this thinking. It shows me he can't be trusted with the future of our church. I want Big Oak to thrive and grow! Nothing personal, Patrick, but I don't have faith in you leading us anymore."

Deacon Joe stepped away from the microphone and Pastor Patrick stepped up.

He said, "Thank you all for being here tonight. I could defend myself against a lot of what Joe said by explaining how he took things out of context and only shared part of what is true. Instead, what I would like to say is very simple. I have led Big Oak for four years with my ideas and had small results. Over the past month, I've allowed God to lead Big Oak through me with amazing results. People are confessing their sins, turning from their wicked ways and calling on the name of the Lord. That's what being the Church is all about. I love each and every one of you no matter how you vote. My future is in God's hands."

Daryl Burchfield said, "Thank you, gentlemen. If you haven't already cast your vote, please mark you ballot, and place it in the offering plate at the front of the church at this time."

People began marking their little, white pieces of paper. Then they made their way up to the front of the church and dropped it into the offering plate. When they had all finished, a man came and took the offering plate away. For the next ten minutes the only sound was a Christian song playing in the background.

Daryl Burchfield stepped back to the mic. "Three of our Church Council members just finished counting the vote and have brought me the results."

Daryl was holding a sealed envelope. He tore it open and removed the slip of paper.

Christy was tightly holding her husband's hand.

The church was on pins and needles. Only a little more than a month ago they were waiting for results of a different kind. The attendance total for High Attendance Sunday. As big as that seemed at the time, it was nothing compared to the consequences today's results would bring.

Daryl said, "The church allows members who are over twelve years old, claim Jesus as their Savior, and are in good fellowship with Big Oak Christian Church the right to vote. Some parents set a higher age for their children to vote. We had 285 votes cast."

There were a little over 400 members before the fire. Once you subtract kids under twelve and some members abstaining from voting 285 was about what was to be expected.

Daryl continued, "By a vote of 231 to 54," everyone was completely silent, "Patrick Spakes...remains pastor of Big Oak Christian Church!"

The church burst into cheers. Christy grabbed her husband and hugged him. Sister Snyder sighed a breath of relief. Daniel and Jamie hugged each other and then their parents. Deacon Joe and several other deacons stormed out the door with their wives.

Daryl gave everyone a minute to settle down then continued, "Eighty-one percent vote in favor of keeping our pastor. Would you like to say a word?"

He stepped to the stage and said, "Thank you, Daryl. Thank you Big Oak for your vote of confidence. Okay, now there is some healing that needs to take place. Please be praying for unity in our church. No matter how you voted, I love you, and God has a ministry opportunity for you here at Big Oak."

He then prayed a prayer from his heart and dismissed his church.

Chapter 22

The following morning the Spakes were sitting down to eat breakfast when Daniel came into the kitchen and said, "I just got a text from JJ. He said Deacon Joe was super upset last night."

Pastor Patrick replied, "Yeah, by the look on his face when we got to church, I'm sure he didn't think there was any way we would reach seventy-five percent of the vote."

Daniel said, "According to JJ, Deacon Joe was yelling at several people until late last night. He heard him say things like 'I thought you had those votes locked up against keeping him' and 'the traitors in this church make me sick.' Some really harsh stuff."

Jamie said, "Why is he so angry with you, Dad?"

He answered, "Sweetheart, you'll learn in life, people have different ideas about how things should be. Especially in church and politics. It's our duty as Christians to know what we believe and why we believe them, and then to live in peace as much as possible with others. We must choose our words and our battles wisely as the Holy Spirit leads us. Deacon Joe and others in the church feel like I am leading the church in the wrong direction. I disagree with them. So, after much prayer and searching the Bible, I had to take a stand. He's upset that the church agrees with me and he's probably a little embarrassed. Now it's my duty as the pastor to reconcile our church with one another and allow God's healing to take place. That's what I'll be preaching on today."

Christy added, "Your dad could be prideful about winning the vote. Instead he is being humble and trying to restore Deacon Joe and those who voted against him."

Daniel inquired, "Is it hard not to celebrate? Do you think the people who voted against you will be there today?"

He answered, "A month ago I probably would have a different attitude. Instead today I find myself praying for those people to be restored to our church. I'm not sure if they will be there today. I hope so. But I don't think anything would surprise me at this point."

Christy said, "I don't know, Patrick. You might not want to let your guard down. I'm not sure this is over yet."

Little did she know how right she was.

68

The Spakes walked into Love Auditorium and were shocked to see how many people were there. He saw Deacon Joe gathered around all of the other men who had called for the vote of confidence. He made his way toward them. He stopped to shake hands and speak with several members on the way, including Buzz McCoy and Daryl Burchfield. As he reached Deacon Joe he shook hands with him and said "It's great to see you here this morning."

Deacon Joe answered, "Patrick, you obviously were more persuasive than we were. To the victor go the spoils."

He said, "I don't see it as a victory, Joe. I see it as our church getting through a tough situation and now we can move forward together. I don't have any hard feelings about what has happened. I believe God has a bright future for all of us."

Deacon Joe said, "Great. Excuse me, I need to get a cup of coffee."

He answered, "Okay, Joe. I'll talk to you later."

He just nodded his head and walked away.

The other men were just as cold to Pastor Patrick as he tried to speak with them. He went away disappointed.

He took the stage and welcomed everyone. He announced that the vote on the budget would be held that evening. Then he opened with a word of prayer.

Sky and Chloe led the worship, which was very good as always. Sky read some scripture before ending the worship set with "Amazing Love."

Pastor Patrick moved into his sermon saying, "I appreciate everyone who is here today. As most of you know, in church, and in life, there are times when people have disagreements on issues. These disagreements can lead to major problems and hurt feelings which, if ignored, can cause problems for years. But if they are addressed in a healthy way, then God can use those tough times to make churches and friendships even stronger. I believe God wants us to live in peace with one another. I also believe He wants us to love each other whether we agree with one another or not. If I have wronged anyone here, I want to ask for your forgiveness. Also, if anyone has wronged me, I want you to know, I forgive you. If God can forgive me, who am I not to forgive others."

His sermon was based on healthy Biblical reconciliation. It was very powerful and many people responded by coming forward. Just as he was closing the altar call, Deacon Joe made his way to the front. Pastor Patrick's spirit leaped.

Was his good friend responding to the Holy Spirit? Was he finally putting their differences aside as he had been fasting and praying for?

"Oh God, please restore our friendship." he silently prayed.

Deacon Joe asked, "May I say a few words?"

Pastor Patrick replied, "Yes, Joe. Go right ahead."

He stepped up and gently said, "Big Oak, I brought up a vote of confidence on Patrick Spakes this past week as you all know. The majority of you voted to keep him as the leader here. I said some pretty tough things. I shared with you I felt Patrick had become a bit of a fanatic. I said that I disagreed with the direction he was leading our church. I prayed last night and I listened to his sermon today."

He paused for a moment. He looked at the congregation and then over at Pastor Patrick.

"I feel like you made a terrible decision and will regret keeping him in leadership here at Big Oak!" Deacon Joe angrily said.

Pastor Patrick's spirit sank.

Deacon Joe continued, "I cannot and will not follow a fanatic! I have invested too much of my life in this church to watch it get wrecked. I am not alone in these thoughts. Several of Big Oak's leaders agree with me. At this point I want to publicly disassociate myself from Big Oak Christian Church. I resign as Head Deacon and I will be transferring churches. I am not alone in this decision. Will everyone who is disassociating from Big Oak please stand."

About fifty men, women, and kids stood up.

He continued, "Anyone who would like to join us is welcome to, or feel free to call me about where we'll be moving. Thank you. I will be exiting now with these fine Christian's. Goodbye."

He watched as Deacon Joe walked down the steps of the stage and down the aisle followed by fifty or so other members. All eight of the deacons who called for the vote of confidence and their families followed him out.

Once they were out of the building, Pastor Patrick made his way to the stage. He was trying to compose himself, but he had never even heard of anything like this happening, much less been a part of something so wild.

He said, "Is there anyone else who needs to say anything or anyone else who needs to leave?"

No one moved.

He continued, "Thank you for being here this morning. I know this is a service you will never forget. I know I won't."

The slight bit of humor allowed everyone a moment of laughter to release some of the nervous energy that had built up.

He continued, "Seriously, we're going to close this morning's service. I hope you are able to come to our gathering tonight in the multi-purpose building on the church campus. Beginning next Sunday we will be meeting there permanently for all services. If you have small kids please go get them from the nursery. I'm going to spend some time in prayer and you are more than welcome to stay also. If you need to go, that's okay. But I want you to know this as you leave, God is in control of everything including our church. Nothing that happened today surprised Him and He has a plan for us. Let's remain obedient to Him!"

He then prayed a brief, but powerful prayer. Over one hundred people remained afterwards to continue in prayer for wisdom, healing, and guidance.

Chapter 23

Pastor Patrick got home about two o'clock. He called a special meeting of the Church Council, the remaining Board of Deacons and the staff members. They met that afternoon at four o'clock. He got some feedback from the leaders and spent some time encouraging all of them. A special vote was held to replace the head deacon position. Tony Lewis was unanimously voted to lead the deacons.

There were about one hundred and forty people at the service that evening. He explained that Big Oak would be meeting the next Sunday morning at nine o'clock in the multipurpose center. If needed, they could add another service at ten-thirty at a later date. He announced Brother Tony as the new leader of the Deacon Board. He also announced a work project for the coming Saturday. He was taking a crew of volunteers to work on the New Hope Church in Westside. They needed people to paint, work on the playground, and renovate some rooms inside their new building. After the announcements, he called for a vote on the budget. It passed overwhelmingly. After the vote was taken and announced, he asked if anyone had anything to say.

Sister Snyder slowly stood up and made her way to the front. He gave the microphone to her.

She said, "Big Oak Christian Church is going through a cleansing right now. It will be a tough time with some deep valleys. There will also be some incredible experiences with God. I've walked this walk. It won't be easy. But God is faithful. He has sent us the right man to lead us through these difficult times. Let's take a moment and pray for him. Anyone who feels led, please come and lay your hands on Pastor Patrick while we pray."

Did she really just call him "Pastor"?

He was surprised and honored.

He knelt down as many members came forward and laid their hands on him and lifted him up in prayer.

After a lengthy prayer time he arose. He thanked the church and then asked if anyone had a testimony to share.

One by one people came forward and shared how God was changing their lives. A teenager confessed he had been having thoughts of suicide, but had been saved and was now getting professional help. One couple shared how God called them to have a yard sale and gave all the proceeds to a food bank in the capital city. Another man admitted he had an addiction, but had repented and asked for forgiveness. He had gotten an accountability partner and was now fighting it.

People just kept coming up sharing how God was moving in their lives. Pastor Patrick loved this so much more than the lukewarm Christian life he had been living and preaching.

He took the stage and shared that he had reserved a spot on the river to have a mass baptism the next Sunday afternoon. Over twenty people had been saved and wanted to follow through in believer's baptism.

He dismissed the service feeling refreshed and excited about what lay ahead.

Chapter 24

Pastor Patrick had asked the church to e-mail him the ways they were coming up with to follow the 3t Challenge. Thursday morning he was reading some of the e-mails he had received from his congregation:

Good Morning Pastor! I wanted to take a minute to share with you what I'm doing to follow the 3t Challenge. I've never read the entire Bible. I knew immediately that's what God was telling me to do. I took the Challenge about two weeks ago and got a one-year Bible reading plan. It's amazing how much I'm enjoying it! I'm learning so much from Genesis right now. Although I know Leviticus and Numbers will be tough, I'm looking forward to the day I can say I have read the whole Bible! -Craig Baker

Hey Pastor! The 3t Challenge is pretty wild! I'm excited about how the kids in our youth group are responding to it. Being the youth minister here has always been good, but the past few weeks have been great! Personally, I've been much more thoughtful about how I spend my 3-t's. It's making me a better Christian, minister, and man! Thanks for challenging us to be more like Jesus! -Clint

Pastor Patrick, The challenge of the 3t's has brought a lot of changes to my family. We have decided to cancel our satellite service and spend the next year without it. As you know, Bobby is six and Shelly is four. We will keep our Christian DVDs for them to watch occasionally, but we really feel like our family time is already improving. We have played outside together more in the past three weeks than we ever did before. Jake and I are growing closer together without the distraction of TV constantly competing for our time. I have to admit when we first decided to do this, we were both really worried about missing too much. Turns out what we were missing was having a real life together. Thank you for being obedient to God and issuing us this challenge. -Marilyn Brown

Pastor, when I first heard you issue the 3t Challenge I figured it was going to be like most things I've heard from sermons all my life. It would be a good idea, but wouldn't really make much of a difference. How wrong I was! God grabbed ahold of Nancy and me, and we have completely surrendered to Him. Everything we have is His. We have prayed about it and are going to sell our house and move into a smaller one! We're now praying about where God wants us to go on our first foreign mission trip. I'll need to talk to you about that soon. Before taking the 3t Challenge I would have told you this is crazy. But we're confident this is what God wants us to do and we're excited! -Jim Sanders

Hey Pastor P!!! Clint has been encouraging us to take the 3t Challenge like you talked about in big church. I decided to take the Challenge and it's tougher than I thought it would be. I realized I was wasting so much time on video games and watching TV. I have started using more of my online time talking to people about Jesus and have started running every afternoon. I already feel better! I'm trying to do better in school too. My mom and dad asked me about the changes they are seeing in me and I got a chance to tell them about Jesus. They don't go to church, but I'm hoping they might give it a shot if I keep following Him. -Cip Ward

Pastor Patrick, I'm on a fixed income so when you issued the Challenge a few weeks back, I felt like I would not be able to participate. It's not that I didn't want to give more money; I just didn't know how I could. Thank you so much for explaining to me that it's not just about giving money. I realize now that it's about giving God my best. So after praying about it, I'm going to begin volunteering in the nursery. I haven't helped in there since my kids were little. They said they would love to have me in the rotation beginning this Sunday. I haven't been so excited for a Sunday to get here in a long time! No offense to you, of course. -Sister Gladys

Pastor Patrick laughed and thought to himself, *No offense taken Sister Gladys.* Then he thought, *I think my people are getting it. God, please help us follow you.*

Chapter 25

Friday night Pastor Patrick had a meeting for all the volunteers going to help New Hope Church get moved into their new building. He explained the agenda for the next day and broke them up into teams. He emphasized how important their words and actions would be. The people in Westside were very different culturally from what his congregation was used to. He warned them against judging the people who lived there. He also told them to be open to learning what God wants to teach them through other Christians they would meet there. They spent some time praying for their trip before dismissing.

The next morning about sixty members of Big Oak caravanned over to Westside. It was a beautiful Saturday morning. Pastor Patrick and Victor Martinez had lined up as many volunteers as they could. There was a lot of work to be done.

The teams divided up between those moving equipment from the old building and those who were going to be renovating and painting the new location.

Victor and Hector met Pastor Patrick and his crew at the old location. They briefed the team on what needed to be moved.

Christy and Jamie went to the new building to get busy painting with the rest of their team. They all worked very hard until noon.

Elizabeth Gonzales and several members of New Hope Church made a delicious lunch for all of the volunteers. Everyone ate together and fellowshipped during lunch. Pastor Patrick was glad to see his Caucasian middle and upper class members laughing and talking with Victor's multicultural lower income church members. Working and eating together quickly broke down many barriers.

When they had finished eating, Victor stood up to speak, "Excuse me. Could I please have your attention? Thank you. I hope everyone has had plenty to eat. We are very thankful for Big Oak coming to help us today. This new facility will be such a blessing to our church and our community." Everyone clapped and cheered.

Pastor Patrick rose from his seat and said, "Thank you, Victor. We really appreciate the lunch and hospitality. We have all made many new friends today. Big Oak has voted to ask you to be our sister church. This will help us support our brothers and sisters in Christ with our time, talents, and treasures. At Big Oak we call it the 3t Challenge."

Victor smiled and said, "Speaking for New Hope, I'm proud to accept your invitation. We will also help Big Oak in any way that we can."

Pastor Patrick said, "Great! Then we begin a new relationship to pray and help each other as God leads us. I have one more thing for New Hope."

He reached into his back pocket and pulled out an envelope. He said, "Big Oak would like to donate some money to your new church. You can use this to help with your after school program, the food closet ministry, or whatever God leads you to do with it."

Victor looked inside the envelope and was shocked to see the amount. Then he said, "We cannot accept this much from you. Your church has already been so generous to us."

He interrupted, "Victor, we are being obedient to what God has led us to do as a church. Please accept our gift and use it for Kingdom purposes."

Victor agreed, hugged Pastor Patrick, and thanked everyone. They dismissed the group to get back to work.

All of the moving had been completed by lunch and they had finished the indoor renovations. The playground was the next project on the list. Some people were finishing up painting the exterior of the church. There was a large space on the front of the building they saved for a mural to be painted.

A teenager from Westside, Theresa, and Jamie were going to paint it together. They had decided on a bright primary color scheme with lots of flowers and a cross. The words "New Hope" would be painted in the mixture of flowers.

The two girls laughed and talked as they worked away. Both girls were very talented artists.

Daniel came by and said, "Do you girls need a real artist to give you a hand?"

Jamie shot back, "Daniel, your only real talent is lifting heavy things!"

Daniel grabbed her and threw her over his shoulder, then he started spinning around in circles. They laughed hysterically while Daniel yelled, "You're right sis! I can lift really heavy things."

He set her down and ran off as she tried to chase him down with her paint brush.

When Jamie returned Theresa said, "Your brother seems really sweet."

Jamie replied, "He's great. I'm really lucky to have him. We have so much fun together."

Theresa continued to paint and then added, "He's pretty cute, too."

Jamie exclaimed, "Oh gross, Theresa!"

Both the girls laughed.

By the end of the day everyone was worn out, but all their hard work was very rewarding. The volunteers from Big Oak headed back to Lost Creek as the sun was setting on a very fruitful day.

Chapter 26

At four o'clock the next day Pastor Patrick called Victor Martinez. The two men had agreed to call and discuss each other's big day.

Victor answered, "Hello."

He said, "Hey, Brother! How was the grand opening of New Hope Church this morning?"

Victor replied, "It was wonderful. Everyone loved the new building. We had eighty-three people here. The praise and worship was great. We're working on getting some more people involved, like we talked about, but this morning was really good!"

He said, "That's great to hear, Victor. Did you get any more volunteers for the after school program?"

Victor answered, "Yes. Dwayne gave a testimony about helping and how rewarding it is. I had three ladies, one man, and a couple of teenagers who talked with me about volunteering. Oh, another man asked me about beginning a twelve step program for people who need help with substance abuse and addictions. He's new to Westside. He said he has led a group in another city, so I'm going to check his references and look at starting a program here."

Pastor Patrick replied, "That's exciting stuff, Victor. I'm so happy everything went well."

Victor said, "Yes. God is so good. Now tell me about your day at Big Oak."

He said, "It was great! We only had a little over two hundred people. That's a lot less than we've been used to lately. I'm not sure if that many families have actually left the church, or if some are just staying away until the drama settles down around here. Regardless, the ones who were here really came to worship. Sky and Chloe, you met them yesterday, led the worship team."

Victor answered, "Yes, I remember them. They are the beautiful young couple engaged to be married."

He said, "They are so musically gifted, but they are even more gifted in leading others into worship. That's why we have offered them the worship leader's position. This morning was amazing. After the worship we had three people, who helped out yesterday, give a short testimony about serving your congregation in Westside. I think it really opened the minds of some of our other members."

Victor said, "We loved fellowshipping with your church."

He said, "We did too, Victor. Remember I told you we were having the baptism at the river?"

Victor answered, "Of course. How did it go?"

He said, "It couldn't have gone any better. We baptized twenty-six people today! The unseasonably warm weather was nice and the water wasn't cold. The best part for me was getting to baptize Daniel."

Victor said, "I'm sure you are a proud Papa."

He said, "Yes, I am. It was very special. Hey, I have a couple of ideas for this summer I want to run by you."

Victor said, "I'm all ears."

He continued, "I liked what you shared with me yesterday about having some church mixers. How about we plan on doing one at the first of the summer here in Lost Creek and then one in Westside toward the end of summer. I also have some members who want to come visit your church on a Sunday. Maybe we could have a member swap one Sunday a month over the summer. You could have some members come over and share testimonies for our church and we'll do the same."

Victor said, "I like that idea. It will give our members a better world view and allow them to share their testimonies, which is always a blessing."

He said, "Maybe one week we can have a pastor swap also."

Victor laughingly said, "I'm not sure Big Oak can handle a passionate Latino in their pulpit."

Pastor Patrick answered, "It will be good for them!"

Victor said, "I'm considering having a revival this summer. What would you think about doing the preaching? I will ask Sky and Chloe to do the worship. I may also do a Vacation Bible School that week. We could use some of your youth to help lead it, if you think they might be interested."

He answered, "I would be honored to speak at the revival. I'm sure several of our students and adults would love to serve and fellowship. We'll work out the details. Hopefully we can have some ministry opportunities for you guys as well."

Victor replied, "That would be fantastic! Some of our people have already taken the 3t Challenge after speaking with your members yesterday. But I'm going to offer the Challenge to our whole church next week. I agree it's a practical way to follow God in our daily lives. It's Biblical and individual, but will affect the entire church."

Pastor Patrick said, "I just really believe that throughout the Bible God asks his people to give Him their best. It's different for each person, but as we each strive to give our best we are all blessed. Most Christians have heard a message on the 3t's. I just kept it simple and tried to make it practical."

Victor answered, "I can see and hear a difference in those who have taken the Challenge in your church. They are actively searching for ways to sacrifice for others in the name of the Lord. That's very rare these days."

He said, "Yes, it is. I feel very blessed that God opened my eyes to my own complacency. Let's pursue these ideas and see where it leads us. We'll pray for the Holy Spirit to lead us where we should go and to do what we should do. Let's pray together before we go."

Victor said, "You lead off, Pastor, and I'll close."

Pastor Patrick began, "Jesus, we praise your name..."

And the two men spent a long time praying for God's wisdom and direction.

Chapter 27

As spring turned into summer lots of changes were taking place. The Spakes sold their house and moved into a nice, but cheaper home. They were able to increase the giving of their treasures this way.

The Lost Creek High School baseball team made it to the district finals. Daniel played great and was voted his team's MVP. He batted .640 and even got to do some middle relief pitching. After the tournament, his coach got very upset when Daniel told him he wasn't playing with the summer travel baseball team. His dad backed up Daniel's decision when the coach appealed to him.

Big Oak Christian Church was being abundantly blessed. Even though they had lost several members with the church split, they were able to give more money than they ever had. Miraculously, they always had plenty.

The gatherings on Sunday nights were running two hundred or more people. Most of them had taken the 3t Challenge. People were searching for ways to give God their time, talents, and treasures. Jarod's car maintenance ministry was a huge success. He had about twelve men, some boys, and two girls helping him. They began with one Saturday a month, but were expanding to every other week. They did car maintenance primarily, but a couple of cars had been donated. They repaired them and gave them to people who were in need.

Tuesday nights became a serving night in the Spakes family. Daniel, inspired by Dwayne in Westside, began giving free guitar lessons. Jamie gave free art lessons to kids, and Christy led a women's aerobics class at the church. Pastor Patrick used Tuesday evenings as a visitation night.

In Westside, things were going great as well. Victor had more help with his church and after school program than he had ever had. The twelve step program was up and running. Hector and Elizabeth had decided to become members of New Hope Church. It was very hard for them, but they knew God was leading them to serve in their own community. Dwayne was still teaching guitar after school and Theresa had started teaching piano. The membership at New Hope had grown to over one hundred and fifty people. Their new building would hold about two hundred.

The first church mixer brought about one hundred and twenty people from Westside to Big Oak on a Saturday night. They ate together and then got ready for worship. The multipurpose center was packed. The worship team was made up of a combination of Sky, Chloe, Dwayne, and Theresa. They did a wonderful job of leading people into worship. Jamie and Daniel were glad to see their friends Dwayne and Theresa. JJ showed up for the service. He didn't tell his dad he was going. He really enjoyed it.

Hector was so happy to see Pastor Patrick. He had missed his pastor over the past few weeks, but he was really a blessing to Victor.

The two pastors preached a message together. They wanted to change things up for the mixer. They took turns teaching about the apostle Paul and how he tried to reach everyone he possibly could, regardless of their race or status, with the good news of Jesus.

After the close of the service, Big Oak had ice cream and desserts for everyone. They really enjoyed the evening of fellowship together. Victor gathered his group and they headed back to Westside about ten o'clock.

Pastor Patrick and Christy were driving Sister Snyder home when she started complaining of dizziness. After talking to her about it for a few minutes, he changed course and headed to the hospital. By the time they reached the emergency room entrance, Sister Snyder was very weak. They rushed her back to a room.

Pastor Patrick and Christy made the decision to activate the church's prayer chain. He also called Victor and asked him to trigger New Hope's prayer chain. In under an hour, hundreds of people were praying for Sister Snyder. Pastor Patrick and Christy prayed in the waiting room. His prayers were mostly for God to ease her suffering and for God's will to be done.

Suddenly he felt led to stop praying for her comfort, but instead pray for her healing. He fought off these thoughts at first thinking he was being selfish, but he couldn't shake the feeling he needed to pray for her to be healed. He was telling Christy how God was leading him to pray when the nurse came out to speak with them.

"Patrick Spakes?" she asked. They were the only people in the waiting room.

Standing up he said, "I'm Patrick Spakes. How is Sister Snyder?"

The nurse replied, "I'm her nurse, Amy. Ms Snyder's heart rate is very slow and she's struggling with her breathing. She was persistent that I give you a message. She said it was very important."

He anxiously said, "Yes, what is it?"

Amy continued, "She said 'This is to build your faith'. Then she said 'John 11:4'. Does that mean anything to you?"

He thought deeply and said, "No. Not off the top of my head. That's about the time Jesus was with Lazarus. But I'll have to look it up."

Christy had her smart phone out and said, "John 11:4 reads 'But when Jesus heard this, He said, 'This sickness is not to end in death, but for the glory of God, so that the Son of God may be glorified by it.'"

He exclaimed, "I knew God was leading me to pray for her healing! She's going to be okay!"

Just as he was saying this the ER doors swung open and another nurse yelled, "Amy, get in here now! We need you!"

A little while later Amy returned. She said, "Pastor, I'm so sorry, but while we were speaking Sister Snyder had a massive stroke. They're rushing her to have a CT scan and calling in an MRI tech to see the severity. It looks really bad. The doctor will be out in a little while to talk with you, but as her power of attorney you need to be thinking about how much care you want her to receive."

Pastor Patrick, in shock, said, "Okay. Thank you."

Amy went back to the ER. He turned to Christy and said, "We've talked about her wishes. Christy, she doesn't want to be on life support. She's told me point blank that she's ready to go be with Jesus and see her late husband Seth. But with the Scripture she shared from the book of John, I'm not sure what to do."

Christy took Patrick's hand and said, "You don't know, but God does. Let's ask Him."

As they were praying Sky, Chloe, and Daryl Burchfield showed up and joined them. A little while later Dr. Johnson came out to see them.

Pastor Patrick said, "David. I didn't realize you were the ER doctor tonight."

Dr. Johnson answered, "Patrick. It's good to see you. I think the last time I saw you was on the golf course. I'm sorry we have to meet this way."

He replied, "Thank you, David. How is Sister Snyder doing?"

Dr. Johnson answered, "Patrick, I've got to be honest. It looks bad. The CT showed a stroke and the MRI confirmed it. At her age I recommend we keep her comfortable and allow nature to take its course. If she has any family members I would call them in. I'm afraid she's not going to make it through the night. Of course if you want us to put her on life support we will. But I wouldn't recommend it."

He answered, "No, don't put her on life support or do anything except keep her comfortable. David, I have to say this out loud even though it sounds crazy. I believe she's going to be alright. I believe God is going to heal her. I don't know why, but I have to share that with you."

Dr. Johnson replied, "I think you're making the right decision. But Patrick, don't get your hopes up for a recovery. She's had a major stroke and she will die. I don't know if it will be tonight, but it will be soon. I've done this long enough to know. Take heart in the fact she has lived a good long life."

He said, "Thank you, David."

Dr. Johnson returned to the Emergency Room.

Pastor Patrick spent the rest of the night crying out to God for Sister Snyder to be healed.

The next morning at 5:08 a.m. Dr. David Johnson burst through the ER doors shouting, "Patrick, I would say you're not going to believe this, but you probably will!"

He was on his knees with his head on a chair, barely awake, but still praying. Everyone else but Christy had left about two a.m. She was asleep in the seat beside him.

Pastor Patrick, startled by the enthusiastic physician, got to his feet. He said sleepily, "What's going on, David?"

Dr. Johnson answered, "Thirty minutes ago Ms. Snyder was your typical ninety-two year old stroke victim. Her heart rate was in the forties, her left side was basically paralyzed, and her scans had confirmed a major brain stroke. Then from out of nowhere, she's hitting the nurse call button and clearly asking if she can have something to drink! We rushed into her room and she's fully coherent, no paralysis, and speaking perfectly fine. I ordered another head CT and there's no sign of a stroke. We repeated the CT a second time to confirm the results: Completely Negative! My first thought was they had mixed up her scans with another patient's. But it was a slow night, and she's the only person they've scanned all night. She's sitting up eating right now. Unbelievable."

Pastor Patrick and Christy were speechless. They were trying to wrap their minds around what was happening.

Dr. Johnson continued, "Pastor, you told me last night she would be healed. You called it. This is medically unexplainable. I've heard and read about miracles. Never really believed them. I figured it was a misunderstanding or a misdiagnosis. This wasn't any of those things. She had a documented debilitating stroke and four hours later is completely healed. I wouldn't believe it if I hadn't seen it with my own eyes."

The reality of the situation was beginning to set in with Pastor Patrick. God had healed Sister Snyder. His prayers had been answered. He asked, "Can I see her?"

Dr. Johnson answered, "Sure! Come on back with me."

As they entered her ER room Sister Snyder was sitting up eating and said, "Good morning, Pastor. You look like a mess. Rough night?"

He just shook his head and laughed.

Dr. Johnson said, "I want to get another MRI before you leave, and an EEG."

Sister Snyder said, "Doctor, I appreciate your concern, but I'm fine. I'm not worried about anything. Rest assured, I'm not immortal. My day will come. God needed to build up my pastor's faith and He chose to use me to do it. I'm blessed."

Dr. Johnson said, "He built up more than your pastor's faith. I'm not too proud to admit it, but I've always felt religion was a crutch for the weak. I've placed my faith in logic and science. What I've seen tonight can't be explained by anything but a miracle."

Sister Snyder smiled and said, "You don't have to give up logic and science to believe in Jesus. My God created logic and science. Miracles happen every day, Dr. Johnson. You just have to slow down to see them."

Dr. Johnson said, "I'll slow down and start looking. Pastor Patrick, when does your church meet?"

Pastor Patrick said, "Sunday mornings at nine. Sunday nights at six. Love to see you there. But let me give you a call this week and we can discuss in more detail what God can mean to your life."

Dr. Johnson replied, "I would like that. Here's my card. I'm free Thursday. I'll give you some privacy."

He said, "Thanks. I'll call you."

Dr. Johnson left the room and Pastor Patrick turned to Sister Snyder and said, "How did you know?"

She smiled and said, "What do you mean?"

He answered, "You had that verse ready. You sent me that message. How did you know you wouldn't die? How did you know this was to build my faith?"

Sister Snyder was thoughtful for a minute then said, "I didn't know. I just said what the Holy Spirit led me to say. I hoped in my heart it was time for me to see my Seth again. Time to meet my Jesus and dance before my Lord. But God had other plans and I'm happy they were for your benefit."

He said, "I have never been led to pray like that before. It was like I was in the presence of God and He told me how to pray. I had no doubt. Will it always be like that now?"

Sister Snyder slightly grinned and said, "Probably not. God works in different ways with each person and each situation. God wants us to simply follow Him. Rarely will He reveal His glory. Don't ever forget how it felt."

He was quiet. Then he said, "When they discharge you, Christy and I will take you home. I love you, Sister Snyder. Selfishly I'm glad you're still here."

She looked away from him with a far off look in her eyes, like she was missing home.

Chapter 28

The story of Sister Snyder's miraculous recovery spread like a wildfire. Pastor Patrick was inundated with phone calls and emails about her supernatural healing. His lunch with Dr. David Johnson led to David receiving Salvation.

Big Oak was growing and the members were very blessed. They were reaching lots of people. Another baptism service was held a few weeks later. Dr. David Johnson was baptized with fourteen other people. Big Oak established several new ministries meeting the members' needs of giving of their time and serving with their talents.

A group of women started a prayer shawl ministry. They knit blankets for the sick or hurting people they heard about. As they knitted the blankets they prayed for that person to experience God's love. A men's group had a team cleaning and mowing elderly people's yards. The youth sold bracelets that had "3t Challenge: time, talents, treasures" printed on them. They took the money they made and donated half to a local food bank. With the other half, they sponsored "Compassion Kids." These are children from all over the world that Compassion International helps release from spiritual, economic, social, and physical poverty.

The Spakes family was involved in a variety of ministries, but kept Monday nights as family night. They would eat together at the kitchen table and then play a game or go to the park.

Daniel missed playing on the summer baseball travel team, but he was happy with his decision. He was really growing spiritually. He spent time each week mentoring some younger guys and also being mentored by Clint. Daniel and Jamie went on the youth summer camp trip and had a blast. God really blessed that week. Daniel was able to pray with several other students for Salvation.

The church staff, Church Council, and Board of Deacons had come up with a building plan. They had unanimously decided to build a three story family life center instead of a new sanctuary. It would have a children's area, a youth center, and a gymnasium for family activities. It would be a great place for families to spend time together and add some healthy living into their busy schedules. The top floor would be a teaching area for people wanting to go into ministry or missions. They would also have a food pantry housed there for those in need.

The Big Oak multipurpose center would get some renovations and two church services would begin as they grew.

Pastor Patrick and Victor switched pulpits one Sunday in July and it was fantastic! Both congregations were blessed.

They prayerfully planned for the revival in August. New Hope would have Vacation Bible School during the week for youth and children. In the evenings Pastor Patrick would preach and Sky and Chloe would lead the worship for the revival. It would run Monday through Saturday. On that Saturday afternoon Victor was going to reserve Redemption Park for the final day of the revival. He hoped this would be a good way to reach the community who might not come to the church building. Pastor Patrick loved the idea, recalling how God had led him to pray for the park on his first visit to Westside.

The Sunday before the revival Big Oak had a wonderful morning service with incredible worship in song and three people receiving Salvation. The new family life center's foundation was coming along nicely. Everyone was excited about the possibilities it allowed families. The gathering that evening was a carryover from the morning service. People were laughing and talking, but almost immediately when the service started the Holy Spirit moved in a mighty way. Pastor Patrick allowed some testimony time for people who had taken the 3t Challenge. He really encouraged his congregation to be in fervent prayer for the revival this week. He shared that while he was really excited about helping their sister church, New Hope, God had revealed to him that trials lay ahead. He had no idea what those trials were, but Westside was a place that needed God's love and He would share it with them no matter the cost.

This was followed by a time of deep prayer. People were begging God to break through barriers and open people's hearts in Westside. They prayed for protection for those serving. They prayed for a spiritual awakening for the lost and revival of the saints, both there and in Lost Creek. People wept and begged God to help them glorify the name of Jesus. Pastor Patrick closed the service and thanked the church for the special offering they had collected the past few weeks. It would go to help New Hope Church with the Vacation Bible School and revival.

As they dismissed this incredible service, no one could have imagined the life altering changes the coming week would bring.

Chapter 29

Monday morning was beautiful. The forecast for the week of the revival was perfect, no rain, low humidity, and mild temperatures. These were very rare conditions for August.

Pastor Patrick, Christy, and Jamie led a caravan of seven cars filled with volunteers to Westside. Daniel had preseason baseball camp. He would drive over to Westside after practice with JJ each day. Pastor Patrick was surprised that Joe was allowing JJ to participate with the revival. JJ told them he had permission if he could ride with Daniel.

The group arrived at noon. The plan was to have VBS from one until five, and then have a community dinner from five to six-thirty. The revival service would go from seven until about nine.

Pastor Victor had lots of volunteers already getting things ready. They would have story time, games, and crafts for the younger kids. The older kids would have a Bible lesson time and games. The whole group would gather for a mass choir practice. They would be performing at the revival in Redemption Park on Saturday afternoon.

Jamie saw Theresa and ran to give her a big hug. She explained to Dwayne that Daniel would be there about two o'clock each day because of baseball practice. She could tell Dwayne was glad to hear his friend would be there.

Pastor Patrick caught up quickly with Victor and they got the volunteers assembled into the main room. Victor's wife, Maria, handed out matching shirts for the volunteers. Victor had everyone's name listed on a white board according to their area of service. Victor went over each area and introduced the volunteers to one another. Then he told them to remember the most important thing this week is to simply love the kids. They may talk or look different, but God's love can break through any barrier they might encounter. After a short prayer, they were dismissed. Kids were lined up according to ages out in front of the church. There were about ninety kids out there. Victor opened the doors and got VBS started.

About two-thirty the older kids' kickball game wasn't going very well. No one was really into it and Pastor Patrick was struggling to keep the kids involved. Daniel and JJ pulled up and ran out to the field.

Daniel yelled "What's up, Dwayne? I'm on your team! JJ you get the other team! Let's play ball!"

Daniel's dad was amazed at the increased energy and fun that was immediately evident. Kids were playing and laughing. Some good natured trash-talking was definitely taking place. For the next hour they all had a blast. Daniel was a natural leader. Pastor Patrick finally had to end the game so they could go to choir practice. He called Daniel and JJ over to him.

"Great job, guys. I was struggling out here until you showed up. How was practice? Did it run late?"

Daniel said, "Dad, you wouldn't believe how tough it was."

JJ said, "Yeah, Pastor P. He ran us 'til I thought I would puke."

Daniel said, "I'm glad you've been pushing me all summer. I think coach gave me a tougher time because I didn't play on the travel team. But I took everything he threw at me!"

He laughed and said, "Aren't you glad you didn't spend all summer on the couch! Good job, guys. You better get in there. I'm proud of both of you."

The boys took off running to the church. Pastor Patrick said to himself, "I wish I had half their energy."

Chapter 30

Monday evening's community dinner and service was good, but the revival service was not nearly as powerful as they had hoped for. Tuesday and Wednesday were about the same. The VBS and evening fellowship meals were going great, but something was missing from the evening services.

Thursday evening Pastor Patrick and Victor Martinez decided to fast and pray during the fellowship meal. They slipped away into one of the classrooms and began praying. They were begging for God to send the Holy Spirit to move among them.

At the close of their prayer Pastor Patrick spoke first, "Victor, I feel like God has been holding back His Spirit. I believe He wants to humble the people from Big Oak, including me. We have had such an outpouring from Him over the summer, I think He is teaching us not to take Him for granted. I believe many of us thought we could box up what we had at Big Oak and bring it here. We weren't being sinful or prideful. God just wants us to realize, He's not a magic act. He wants to move in a different way and we need to adjust to His leading. Tonight I want to change up our approach and allow God more room to lead us."

Victor said, "I will be praying for the Holy Spirit to have the freedom to lead us. Patrick, I'm disappointed no one is responding to the altar calls, but this has still been a very good week. I agree with you that it feels like God is holding Himself back from us. I desperately want this community to experience the love of God as powerful as I did the day we first met."

He replied, "Victor, we are being as obedient as we know how to be. I believe God knows that and He wants to spiritually grow us in our dependence on Him; not depending on a program or a catch phrase. I'm excited about getting to share the truth with others tonight! We have done all we can. Now let's rest in the knowledge that it's God's role to draw people to Himself as we are obedient to Him. Let's go fellowship with everyone for a little while before service."

The men returned to the group. Everyone seemed to really be enjoying the fellowship dinner.

At seven o'clock Pastor Victor welcomed everyone. Sky and Chloe then opened with a very powerful worship song. The congregation began to feel God moving. This was exactly what Pastor Patrick had hoped for, which made his next move shocking, even to himself. As the song came to an end he stepped forward to the stage. The worship set was supposed to have four songs and he hated to break the spirit that had fallen over the assembly.

Sky continued to softly play as Pastor Patrick said gently, "God is so good. This is unplanned, but I feel the Lord wants someone to share a prayer request. I don't know who or what it is about, but I feel strongly that someone needs prayer. If it is you, please come forward."

No one moved.

He couldn't get past the feeling and said once again, "If anyone has a prayer request that God is leading you to share with this church, please don't be fearful. God wants you to share your need. Don't be afraid."

After another minute that seemed like an eternity, Wanda Williams stepped out into the aisle and made her way to the front of the assembly. She was a sweet, soft-spoken lady. She had tears streaming down her cheeks as she said, "Many of you know my son, Julius. He's moved off to the capital city and he's messed up. I love him with all my heart, but I'm afraid he's too far gone. When the Pastor said someone needs prayer, I knew he was talking about Julius. I did my best raising him. Without a miracle I'm scared he'll be dead soon. He's a good kid who's made some bad decisions." Then she broke down sobbing.

Pastor Patrick had his arm around her and she buried her face in his chest. Christy and Elizabeth rushed up immediately to help comfort her. He leaned over to the mic and said, "I would like some ladies to come and lay hands on this sweet mom who obviously loves her child. We're going to pray for Julius. I don't know him, but God does. And God is in the business of redeeming lost souls!"

They began to cry out to God for Julius, but many who knew him didn't believe there was any hope.

After a wonderful time of prayer Sky and Chloe continued to lead worship in song. The Holy Spirit was moving in the hearts of people.

Pastor Patrick preached a powerful sermon. This week he had taught on the cross. Tonight's message had been on how forgiveness was made possible by the perfect sacrifice of Jesus. All week long a few people would come in late during the service. Some would even show up toward the very end of the sermon. Tonight was no exception. About three people had come in over half way through the message. As he gave the invitation to come forward and pray, Sky came up and began to play his guitar. Once again no one moved.

Then a young man who had come in toward the end of the service began to make his way to the front. Pastor Patrick was excited to see someone finally coming forward. But he noticed everyone who had looked up from praying were poking those around them and whispering. By the time the young man was up to the front the whole congregation was stirring and whispering.

The young man looked at Pastor Patrick and said, "I'm Julius. I don't know why I came here tonight. Something inside of me told me to. Pastor, I've done some really bad things. Is there any hope for me?"

Chapter 31

Pastor Patrick stood for a moment in stunned silence. As his thoughts caught up with him, he realized he was right in the middle of a miracle. He looked the young man in the eyes and said, "Yes, Julius, there is hope for you."

Julius's eyes welled up and his voice cracked as he replied, "But Pastor, you don't understand. I've done some really bad stuff."

He said, "Julius, no matter what you have done, God wants to forgive you."

Julius replied, "Yeah, Pastor, but I just don't know. I'm a user. I use drugs. I use women. I use people. I don't think there's any way God could forgive somebody like me."

He asked Julius, "Do you want to be saved? Do you want to turn from the way you're going and follow God?"

Julius replied, "Yes, Pastor, I do. More than anything. But I think I need to go clean myself up and then come back. He don't want me like this."

He said, "Julius, God wants you exactly the way you are right now. You can't go and clean yourself up enough to deserve to be saved. It's like this Julius. Let's say to be saved, people have to jump to the moon. You can train however you want, but ultimately for Salvation you have to jump all the way up to the moon. You can lift weights, run bleachers, and do all the calf raises you want. Now some people would do much better than others would. An NBA player would do a lot better than me, but absolutely no one would be able to make that jump, would they?"

Julius replied, "No."

He continued, "But what's impossible for us is possible for Jesus. You see Julius, Jesus did what was impossible for us to do."

He paused to let the idea sink in and then said, "That's what Jesus does. But what he did was a lot harder thing than jumping to the moon. He paid off our debts that we couldn't pay. He had to come to earth, live a perfect life, die a sacrificial death, and conquer death by raising up from the grave. He never sinned, but He was punished to pay for our sins. He did that so you can have Salvation, Julius."

Julius began to weep and collapsed to his knees. Pastor Patrick knelt with him. The two men held onto one another as Julius cried out to God.

Men and women flooded forward crying out for their loved ones to be saved.

Thursday night at New Hope went late. Fortunately, the Spakes were staying Thursday and Friday night with the Gonzales family. Baseball practice ended Thursday, so Daniel and JJ were able to sleep in and recover. It had been an exhausting week for everyone.

The boys slept until ten o'clock the next morning. Everyone gathered for breakfast excited about the previous night's miracle. Julius had really been broken by God. After the service dismissed he stayed to talk with Pastor Patrick and Victor. Julius explained how he had run out of drugs and was looking to score some, when a guy pulled a gun on him and took his cash. Knowing he couldn't get any for free he decided to drive over to Westside and try to get some. He knew they would be dealing in Redemption Park. He was hoping he would know someone who would hook him up. But he made up his mind on the drive over that he would rob or kill for them if he had to. As he drove into Westside something told him to go to the elementary school. The mural on the church building caught his eye.

He didn't know why, but he pulled into the parking lot and felt drawn to go inside.

Victor asked him what time he was robbed? Miraculously, it was the exact same time his mom was asking for prayer for him.

Everyone around the table listened as Pastor Patrick shared the story.

After explaining more to Julius about Christ and Salvation, Pastor Patrick and Victor told Julius he's also going to have to own up to what he's done.

They asked him to make a list of all the crimes he had committed and people that he had wronged as best he could remember. They explained he would need to start making restitution as God led him. He agreed to do that and then asked if that was part of his Salvation.

Pastor Patrick emphasized to him again that good works are not a part of God's saving grace. He explained to Julius that when we are saved, God calls us to turn from the way of the world and to follow Jesus. He told him that is what following God is all about. It means thinking about and doing the things God wants us to do. Not to get Salvation, but because we are saved we desire to change and be more like Jesus. After talking to Julius for a long time, they took him home where his mom was waiting up for him.

After he finished sharing, they all got ready and headed up to New Hope for the last day of VBS. The weather had been perfect all week. Daniel and

96

JJ were glad to be able to attend the whole session today. It went great and everyone had a good time. Julius was there. He and Daniel had a good talk about their faith.

The evening fellowship meal was wonderful. Everyone from Big Oak had been accepted into the community of believers at New Hope. As the meal ended and the revival service time approached, Pastor Patrick noticed some rough looking young people outside in the parking lot. For some reason his mind jumped back to the Lord telling him this week would bring great trials. He rushed to get Victor. He prayed silently for God to protect them and for this revival to not be ruined by any trouble.

Victor and Pastor Patrick got to the front of the church just as Julius walked up to the group. He gave them fist pumps and hugs. These were some of his friends from Westside he had invited to the revival. He introduced them to Victor and Pastor Patrick. The two men were relieved that there wasn't any trouble, and excited Julius was proudly spreading the news of his Salvation.

New Hope church was filling up just before seven o'clock. The news of Julius being saved and the outpouring of the Holy Spirit had people inviting all their family, friends, and neighbors to attend. Victor welcomed the capacity crowd. By the time Sky began the service there was standing room only in the church. After an upbeat praise song, a video began playing behind them.

Dwayne had put together pictures of the VBS events and revival set to some fun music. Everyone enjoyed seeing the images from the wonderful week. They all clapped and cheered as the presentation ended.

Sky began to play softly as Wanda Williams took the microphone and read aloud from her Bible, "Luke 7:12-15 says 'Now as He approached the gate of the city, a dead man was being carried out, the only son of his mother, and she was a widow; and a sizeable crowd from the city was with her. When the Lord saw her, He felt compassion for her, and said to her, 'Do not weep.' And He came up and touched the coffin; and the bearers came to a halt. And He said, 'Young man, I say to you, arise!' The dead man sat up and began to speak. And Jesus gave him back to his mother.'"

She closed her Bible and said, "I know exactly how this woman feels. While my son, Julius, wasn't physically dead, he was very, very close. I feared hearing the news of his death every day. Last night Jesus gave him back to me! Praise the Lord!"

She made her way back to her seat as Chloe and Sky moved the congregation into a powerful time of worship. Pastor Patrick hated for the worship in music to end. People all over the room were crying, kneeling in prayer, and praising God.

He stepped up and softly prayed for the Lord to speak through him this evening. He began his sermon on Jesus's final words on the cross. He explained the different phrases Jesus spoke as He was hanging on the cross. By the time he got to "Father, into your hands I commit my spirit" the Holy Spirit had fallen powerfully on the crowd. During the invitation people all around the room were crying out to God. Victor was praying with some of the young men Julius had invited. Christy and Maria were praying with some ladies. Hector and Dwayne were talking with some other young men. Daniel and JJ were praying with each other. Theresa and Jamie were praying with some teenage girls. Lives were being changed and souls were being redeemed.

Chapter 32

Friday night's service went late into the evening. Everyone slept in Saturday morning after the wonderful Friday night revival meeting. The Saturday service at Redemption Park was scheduled to begin at four p.m. Victor and Maria came over to Hector's for lunch.

Everyone was busy sharing their stories from the glorious night.

JJ interrupted the group, "Hey, everyone! I have something I want to tell you. Last night, during the service, I prayed to be a follower of Jesus. I have been talking to Daniel about this all week. He helped me realize, I don't have to be embarrassed about my relationship with God or worry about what people think. I did pray a prayer when I was really young, but I only did it to make my parents happy. I'm so excited to actually want to follow and obey God! It's so much more fulfilling!"

Everyone clapped and gave JJ hugs of congratulations.

At two o'clock they all headed over to New Hope Church to pick up the sound equipment. Then they went to Redemption Park to set up for the service.

As four o'clock drew near everything was all set. The sound checks went good and a large crowd was gathering. Church members, invited guests, and curious people from the park were all gathering around.

Victor welcomed everyone with a short prayer. Sky and Chloe then kicked up the worship. They had Dwayne helping on the electric guitar and Daniel filled in on the drums. Pastor Patrick thought to himself as he watched Daniel, *That boy can play anything!*

The entire VBS choir made their way up to the set next. They filled in around the band and sang the two songs they had been working on all week. It was fantastic!

The music was great and the crowd continued to grow. After the VBS choir was finished some people gave short testimonies of what Jesus meant to them. Hector Gonzales, Theresa, and Julius all got up and shared a word about their walk with God. It was powerful to hear everyday believers sharing their faith.

The next set of worship was slower and more intense building into a passionate outpouring of praise sweeping the crowd. Pastor Patrick was praying fervently for the Holy Spirit to move in a mighty way. He took the stage as the band was finishing their final song. As they exited the stage he prayed for God to be with this assembly. Then he began his sermon.

"Westside, it is wonderful to be in Redemption Park this evening. I want to thank New Hope Church for sponsoring this event. How many of you know how Redemption Park got its name? I did a little homework and found the origins of this unique park. In 1945, the capital city was growing like crazy at the end of World War Two. They needed a larger city dump and decided to use this area where we stand today. One elderly man, CJ Hutson, loved this area and thought it was a horrible idea to ruin this beautiful place with garbage. He was wealthy and bought as many acres as he could around here. He spent all he had acquiring this land. Once the city realized he had bought so much land and wouldn't sell it to them, they changed locations and moved the plans for the dump to another side of the city. For the next twenty years, Lost Creek was where the city dump was located. Some of you say the rich folks over there in Lost Creek stink. Well, now you know why!"

Everyone laughed.

He continued, "Brother Hutson, as he was known to his church friends, decided to name this Redemption Park, because it was land that had been redeemed. Upon his death he donated it to the city of Westside, which at the time was basically a post office, school, and general store."

He paused for a moment then continued his message.

"This story of Redemption Park, where we stand today, illustrates a more important event that took place about two thousand years ago. God had created Man, but Man chose sin over God. Being perfect in His justice, God couldn't just overlook Man's sin. But God loved Man so much that He sent His Son Jesus to pay the price for our sins. John 3:16 says 'For God so loved the world, that He gave His only begotten Son, that whoever believes in Him shall not perish, but have eternal life.' Every man and woman is guilty of sin. Romans 3:23 says 'For all have sinned and fall short of the glory of God.' Think about it. Have you sinned even one time? Then you don't deserve to be with God. I know I sure don't. Romans 6:23 begins, 'For the wages of sin is death.' You see we all have earned death. But because of His grace and mercy, God sent His Son to redeem all who call on the name of Jesus in faith. Romans 6:23 finishes up by saying, 'But the free gift of God is eternal life in Christ Jesus our Lord.'

Where we see a dump, God sees a beautiful park. Where we see a wasted life, God sees a beautiful soul He wants to save and redeem. God paid the price for your Salvation and offers it freely to you. 1st John 1:9 says, 'If we confess our sins, He is faithful and righteous to forgive us our sins and to cleanse us from all unrighteousness.'"

Pastor Patrick continued to share the truth of God's love with the huge crowd. He then moved into a time of invitation.

As Sky lightly played "Come Just as You Are" people from all around responded to the invitation.

Fortunately, Victor had lined up several of his Christian friends to come to the service and work as volunteers if needed. And they were needed! All of them. There were so many responding to the call to be saved, volunteers were talking to several people at once. It was as powerful as the previous night, but with a much larger crowd.

Two hours after they had begun the invitation they were finally finishing up. It was as if God had poured Himself out and people were basking in His love. Victor was going to be very busy following up with everyone. He wasn't greedy though and directed some people to speak with his friends from other churches. Victor was more concerned about the lost being saved than adding members to his church.

Pastor Patrick made his way over to Daniel. He said, "Hey, Daniel. Great job on the drums tonight. You guys really brought it!"

Daniel smiled and answered, "Hasn't this been a spectacular week, Dad. It's amazing how rewarding it is to serve God."

He agreed, "Yeah, it's been an incredible week. I'm really proud of you. You have made a big difference in the lives of a lot of people."

Daniel replied, "It's so awesome, Dad. Seeing people who have almost given up on life, and then Jesus opens their eyes and it's like they just come alive! I don't think I'll ever get tired of that!"

He said, "It is amazing. Daniel, don't forget how you feel right now. Life has a way of making you forget great moments like this. I love you, Son."

Daniel replied, "Love you, too. And I'm really proud that you're my dad."

They hugged and then headed over to help clean up.

Chapter 33

It was almost dark as they loaded up the chairs and sound system. They went over to New Hope Church and unloaded the equipment. Everyone was talking about all the blessings they had experienced this week.

Pastor Patrick, Victor, and Hector all agreed to meet the following Thursday for lunch. Christy, Maria, and Elizabeth were talking about how great the week had gone. Jamie, Theresa, and Chloe were all laughing about something. Dwayne, Sky, Julius, JJ, and Daniel were talking and laughing also.

Finally at 10:09, Pastor Patrick said, "All right everyone from Big Oak, time to load up."

Everyone hated to leave, but they gave their hugs and handshakes, and then hopped into their cars. Pastor Patrick, Christy, and Jamie were leading. Sky and Chloe followed them, and Daniel and JJ brought up the back.

The boys got caught at a stop light toward the edge of town. Pastor Patrick was slowing down to let them catch up when his phone rang. It was JJ.

He answered, "Hey, JJ. I'm slowing down to let you catch up."

JJ said, "Hey, Pastor P, we're starving. Is it cool if we stop at the gas station right here and grab some snacks?"

He hesitated then said, "Yeah. That will be fine. Don't waste any time and call me as soon as you're back on the road."

JJ said, "You got it, Pastor P!"

Then he hung up and said, "Daniel, your dad is cool! Pull in, I'm starving!"

When Pastor Patrick hung up he had an uneasy feeling about the boys stopping by themselves.

The boys went into the gas station. Daniel grabbed a milk, peanut butter crackers, and a bag of almonds. JJ grabbed a soft drink and a candy bar.

JJ said, "Daniel, you eat way too healthy! You need to enjoy some of this delicious sugar!"

Daniel laughed and said, "No thanks, Bro. This will get me through the trip home. Then we can get some real food."

As the two boys exited the store, four Hispanic teens approached them. One of them stared at Daniel. The others looked over JJ. Daniel nodded to the guy and said, "Hey, man."

The teen answered, "You're not from around here are you?"

Daniel said, "No. We're visiting some friends over here in Westside."

The teen said, "Not too many people come to visit Westside."

Daniel and JJ were getting worried about where this was heading.

The teen continued, "I think I've seen you before. Did you hang out at Redemption Park tonight?"

Daniel said, "Yeah man. I was playing the drums with the band. We've been up here all week helping New Hope Church with their revival."

The teen answered, "That's a good thing you're doing. My little cousin hung out over there all week. She really liked it."

Daniel said, "That's great. We had lots of kids there."

The teen asked, "So why did you do it? Why did you come to Westside to help those poor kids? Do you pity them? Or does it make you feel better about being a rich kid?"

Daniel said, "Honestly, we did it because it's what we felt like Jesus wanted us to do. It's not pity because some of the friends I made here are going to come visit Lost Creek and hang out with us."

The teen said, "Lost Creek, huh? That's about what I figured. Hey man, what was going on at the park tonight? It was crazy out there. I saw some hard-core dudes on their knees and crying. What's up with that?"

Daniel said, "God showed up. Best thing I can tell you is that God loves people. Westside. Lost Creek. Wherever. We have to roll, but swing by New Hope Church over by the school. Ask for Victor Martinez. He'll hook you up with all you want to know."

The teen said, "Victor, huh? I hear he's a solid dude." Then he smiled and added, "Get outta here Lost Creek, before I decide you're not welcome."

Daniel looked him in the eye and said, "Go see Victor. You won't regret it."

Daniel and JJ got in the car. As Daniel pulled out of the parking lot, JJ called Pastor Patrick.

He answered, "Hey, JJ. I was getting worried. What took you so long?"

JJ said, "Well, Pastor P, your son is trying to get all of Westside saved before we leave."

He smiled and said, "I can't wait to hear the story. Are you guys headed this way now?"

JJ replied, "You would have been proud of him, Pastor P! Yeah, we're headed home. Daniel said to tell you we're following the same route around the capital city we have all week. And I'll add he's driving very safe with his hands at ten and two, and going under the speed limit. I feel like I'm riding with my grandma."

He replied, "Great, JJ. You two be safe and we'll see you soon."

JJ laughingly said, "Okay, Pastor P! I'll take good care of your boy! We need his arm and bat this spring for a championship!"

Pastor Patrick said bye and hung up.

Daniel said, "I can't believe my dad lets me hang out with a juvenile delinquent like you."

JJ laughed and said, "Man, your dad knows I'm a good influence on you. Hey, what did you think about those dudes at the store? I thought that one was gonna jump you there for a minute!"

Daniel said, "I know! He was staring me down. I was praying hard!"

JJ said, "Lucky you had me with you. I think I intimidated them."

Daniel said, "Yeah, right. With those little pop guns for arms I bet they were worried!"

JJ flexed his arm for Daniel and said, "This arm is gonna carry us to state this year."

Daniel said, "I sure hope so. We should be pretty solid. If we can score a few runs, I think our pitching will hold up."

JJ said, "Yeah, looks like you're gonna get in the rotation. That's cool."

Daniel replied, "I think my control is getting better. Hey, back to those guys at the store. Do you think they'll go talk to Victor?"

JJ said, "Man, who knows. I hope so. They looked pretty rough."

Daniel replied, "Yeah, but look at everything God did this week! Who would have thought we would get to see so many miracles? I think it would be awesome if that guy gets in touch with Victor and gets saved!"

At that very moment a deer ran right in front of Daniel's car! He swerved to avoid it but there was another one following. He rammed the second deer and it hit his bumper, then flew up and crashed into the front window. Daniel hit the brakes, but lost control and the car slid sideways into an old oak tree.

When the dust finally settled, one boy was unconscious with a broken arm. The other was dead.

Chapter 34

Pastor Patrick, Christy, and Jamie rushed to the hospital. They had just gotten a phone call informing them Daniel had been in a car wreck. The details were sketchy, but by the time they got to the emergency room they had pieced together that one of the boys had a broken arm and the other was in critical condition. All of them were praying that it wasn't as bad as it sounded. As he drove, Christy and Jamie were both calling everyone they could, trying to get some news. When they arrived they ran into the ER. He entered the waiting room with Christy and Jamie right on his heels. The first thing he saw was Joe sitting in a chair with his face in his hands, weeping.

He walked over to him and said, "Joe, I'm so sorry."

Joe looked up through his tears. He dropped his face back into his hands and sobbed a few more times. He placed his hand on Joe's shoulder. Joe composed himself and stood up. He embraced Pastor Patrick in a hug.

Then he softly said, "No, Pastor. I'm sorry."

For a moment he was confused. It was as if time stopped. His mind was trying to process the news, but it wouldn't register. Then it crashed in like a tidal wave.

He let go of Joe and turned to Christy. She knew by his look it was bad. She began saying "No" over and over as he took her into his arms. At first she fought him. Then she collapsed into him weeping.

Jamie stood watching, not realizing yet that her young, talented, energetic brother was gone.

She said loudly through growing tears, "What is it? Where's Daniel? Why aren't we going back to see him? We need to find out what's wrong! Somebody tell me what's going on!"

Her dad realized Jamie was yelling and turned and pulled her into his and Christy's embrace.

Jamie exclaimed, "I want to see Daniel" several times as the truth slowly sank in. Then she broke down sobbing.

Dr. David Johnson happened to be the ER doctor on duty. He got word Pastor Patrick and his family had arrived and immediately went out to speak with them. It was obvious as he entered the waiting room with his nurse they knew about Daniel. He walked over, put his hand on his pastor's shoulder, and said, "Bring your family and follow me. We have a private room for you."

Dr. Johnson and the nurse guided the Spakes back to a family conference room. They were all crying uncontrollably.

After giving them some time to compose themselves Dr. Johnson said, "I'm sorry for your loss."

Pastor Patrick looked up and said, "Tell me David. I have to hear it."

Dr. Johnson answered, "Daniel's dead. He was killed in the car accident."

Sounds that can only come from people grieving the loss of a loved one filled the room.

Finally they composed themselves enough for Dr. Johnson to continue.

Through bloodshot teary eyes he asked, "David, what happened?"

Dr. Johnson explained, "From what I can piece together from the EMTs and police on the scene, the boys hit a deer. It doesn't look like they were speeding or driving recklessly. It sounds like Daniel probably swerved to miss one deer and hit another which caused him to lose control and hit a tree. They were both wearing their seat belts and the airbags deployed. Unfortunately, the side impact snapped Daniel's neck and he died instantly."

Everyone lost control once more, wailing for their beloved son and brother.

Chapter 35

The next day Big Oak Christian Church was supposed to be celebrating New Hope's revival. Instead it was a time of mourning.

The Spakes weren't in attendance. The student minister, Clint O'Dell, led the service. It was primarily a time of prayer for the Spakes family and mourning the loss of Daniel.

They decided to have Daniel's funeral on Thursday, and asked Victor to perform the eulogy. They originally planned the service to be held in the high school basketball gym. After careful thought, the school principal asked them to move it to the baseball field, where there would be much more space.

Both Patrick and Christy had lost their parents earlier in life. He was an only child and Christy had a brother and sister. Her older brother was twice divorced without any kids. Her sister was married and had a twelve year-old son and ten year-old daughter. Christy's family stayed in a hotel and agreed to meet at the service.

Thursday morning, Jamie walked into the kitchen where her mom and dad were discussing the order of the service with Victor and Maria.

Jamie looked at Victor and said, "I would like to say something at Daniel's funeral today. Would that be alright?"

Christy said, "Honey, are you sure you want to stand up in front of everyone and speak? It's going to be a very emotional day."

Jamie answered, "I don't think I have any more tears left, Mom. This is something really important to me. I promise I'll be okay."

Victor said, "Of course you can speak, as long as it's okay with your parents."

The Spakes eventually agreed to allow her to share.

It was an overcast mild late August day. A cold front had moved in and it was in the seventies, which was unusually cool for this time of year. As the Spakes exited the car and walked to the baseball stadium they were amazed at how many people were in attendance.

Daniel's coffin was at home plate. Beside it was a huge picture of him in his baseball uniform. Daniel's guitar, baseball bat, and Bible were placed all around the picture of him. The family would be sitting in a section of seats reserved down the first base line.

107

The stands were completely full. Overflow seating had been set up from the infield back. Those seats were filled and there was standing room only behind them in the outfield that was filled with people. A lectern was set up behind the casket where the speakers would stand.

Sky and Chloe were located over by first base. He was seated playing "Amazing Grace" softly on his acoustic guitar. Chloe was sitting beside him holding a cordless mic.

The Spakes family had asked for people to donate to the New Hope Church after school program in Daniel's name, rather than buying flowers. Still, there were several beautiful arrangements around his casket.

The baseball team was seated along the third base line. They wore their school baseball uniforms. JJ was there with his arm in a cast. Beside him a seat was left empty with Daniel's baseball cap placed in it.

Jamie noticed a whole section in the outfield filled with their Westside friends. Dwayne, Theresa, and Julius were all together. There were also several of the students they had worked with during VBS only a week ago. She was happy they were there.

Chloe joined Sky and sang the first verse of "Amazing Grace". Victor then stepped up to the lectern and said a short prayer. Daniel's baseball coach came up and talked about what a great leader and teammate Daniel had been.

Next Clint O'Dell spoke about the Christian leader Daniel had become. He emphasized Daniel not only went to church, but strived to follow God in all that he did. Victor came back to the lectern and announced they had another speaker not listed on the program.

Victor said, "Jamie Spakes, will you please come up and share what is on your heart."

As Jamie made her way out to the lectern she didn't experience any fear. She was focused on what she had to say and was in total peace.

She stepped up to the mic and began, "I'm Daniel's little sister, Jamie. I have had the privilege to live all my life with the most wonderful brother in the whole wide world. It's a tragedy that he is no longer with us. Daniel was a natural leader and positively influenced so many people. After I found out about the accident, I was devastated. When I got home from the hospital I went into Daniel's room, laid on his bed, and cried myself to sleep. When I woke up, I began to look around at his stuff. He would have yelled at me if he would have caught me snooping."

Everyone laughed. Jamie took a moment to gather herself and continued, "There was a pile of stuff Mom and Dad brought home that was recovered from the wreck. I ran across Daniel's journal. I saw him writing in it all the time. It is his personal thoughts, but I feel like I should share one particular journal entry with you today. I think Daniel would want me to.

So here it is: 'August 10th: I'm so excited about this month! Baseball practice starts on Monday and I can't wait! I didn't play summer travel ball and while I missed it, God really used this summer to grow me spiritually. Clint is teaching us so many things about Jesus and how we can be more like Him. I'm doing my best to submit to the 3t Challenge. I'm teaching some guys to play the guitar on Tuesdays. Dwayne can be thanked for that one! I'm trying to think of some way to give more of my treasures to others. I gave JJ some money for a speeding ticket he got. I told him he needed to tell his dad about it. Not sure if he will.'"

Everyone laughed again. JJ smiled.

Jamie said, "Sorry, JJ, I guess if you haven't told him yet, your dad knows now."

Then she continued reading from Daniel's journal, "I was reading what Paul wrote to the Corinthians: 'Whether, then, you eat or drink whatever you do, do all to the glory of God.' That really spoke to me. I think that means if I'm playing baseball, playing my guitar, or just hanging out, I should do it in a way that honors God. Instead of just trying to keep the rules and get by with what I can, I should live on purpose for Jesus. What a more rewarding life that would be. I had a good talk with my dad again about the call to ministry. I'm still not sure where God might lead me, but I'm as submitted to Him as I think I can be. Dad has been so great these past few months. I'm so lucky to have a mom and dad who really love me. I hope Jamie continues to pursue God's will for her life. I have to be sure to tell her how important it is, at her age, to listen to God and obey him. I'm pumped about the coming week at Westside. I'm praying God will use me in a special way to impact peoples' lives for His glory! If I don't do anything else in my life, I hope I get to tell as many people as possible about the love and forgiveness Jesus offers everyone. Three weeks 'til I'm a senior! Big year coming up. Okay gotta close this out. JJ's coming over to run sprints with me. Gotta get ready for our senior year baseball championship!" Jamie paused and added, "At the bottom Daniel wrote '3t Challenge- tell somebody!'"

Jamie stopped and looked around at the many faces staring back at her. Then she said, "Daniel said to tell someone, so I am. The 3t Challenge is giving God your time, talents, and treasures to use as He leads you to by the Holy Spirit. But to be able to use these things for God, you first have to be a follower of Him. You see, God so loved the world that He sent His only Son that whoever believes in Him will not perish but have eternal life. If you really believe in Him, then you will follow Him. Just as my brother did. And if you believe and follow him then someday you will get to see Daniel again. And even better than that you will be able to be with Jesus in Heaven. While we should mourn Daniel's death today, we should also celebrate Daniel's eternal life with God. He wanted you to know. And now you do."

With that Jamie turned and made her way back to her seat.

Chapter 36

Victor came back to the lectern. He said, "Thank you, Jamie. I know your brother would be very proud of you today. Jamie is right about Daniel wanting as many people to know about the forgiveness and eternal life that Jesus offers to everyone. I don't feel led to have a public invitation, on such an emotional day, for anyone to declare if you receive Salvation today. If you would like to speak with someone about your Salvation please call or visit Big Oak or New Hope Church. Both church's contact information is in your funeral program. I can assure you, Daniel would not want you to attend his funeral service without hearing that Jesus loves you and wants you to have an abundant life with Him."

Victor looked over the crowd and continued, "Daniel Spakes was a natural leader. He influenced people without even realizing he was doing it. His mom and dad have told me many stories this week about him. He was a gifted athlete and musician. When he was playing on his first grade baseball team, he hated to lose. While most kids were playing in the dirt, Daniel would get their attention and explain what to do if the ball was hit to them. His coach said it was like having an extra coach on the field. One time, in a tie ball game, Daniel grabbed a bat and was at the plate before anyone realized he was batting out of turn. Thinking it was just an error, Daniel's coach went and got the six year-old and told him it wasn't his at-bat. Daniel replied, 'I know it's not my turn, but I'm a better batter than him and I want to win.'"

Everyone laughed.

Victor continued, "I didn't meet Daniel until last spring when he had fully committed his life to Jesus. Daniel and I had some wonderful conversations about many things. He had a heart for people and really cared for everyone he came in contact with. The Bible says David was a man after Gods own heart. I believe Daniel Spakes had that same desire. I realize each one of us had a different relationship with Daniel, but I bet if I asked each one of you if Daniel influenced you, the answer would be 'Yes.' Whenever a young person dies, especially such a good young man, we usually ask 'why would God allow this to happen?' I've asked that question many times, including several times this week. I can't explain the mind of God or attempt to give you a reason other than, God is perfect, and God's will is perfect. He loves us, but He doesn't promise us that we will get what we want. In fact, He says plainly that following Him will be difficult and cost us everything. If you, like me, have questioned why God would take Daniel this early, let me tell you a story that may give you a little peace.

Daniel and I were talking last week during VBS. We were discussing how tough his baseball practices were going. He said God was giving him strength he didn't realize was available. Then he turned our conversation to a different area. He asked me if I had ever struggled for the Lord and been given extra strength. I told him that I had, at times, experienced God's extra power to continue through struggles. Then Daniel said something I won't ever forget.

He said, 'I hope God uses me in a way that affects lots of people for Him. I hope I can stand before Him and hear Him say to me, 'Well done my good and faithful servant.' Then Daniel said, 'I can't wait to see Jesus face to face and really worship Him!'

I thought those words were impressive when I heard them. I didn't realize how powerful they really were until this week. Mourn losing Daniel today, but know in your heart that he is celebrating right now in the presence of Jesus!"

Victor finished the eulogy and then Sky and Chloe sang one of Daniel's favorite songs, "How Great is Our God". It was powerful. People were weeping and praising God with the knowledge Daniel was worshipping the Lord face to face.

After the song the baseball team stood and walked to either side of Daniel's casket. They raised it up and carried it to the waiting hearse.

The graveside service was private for family and invited friends. It was a simple service. As Victor spoke, rain gently began to fall from the sky.

Victor finished and dismissed the family first. Pastor Patrick stood and walked to his son's casket. He placed his right hand on the cold hard coffin. As he tore himself away from his son's casket he felt as if a part of him had died.

Chapter 37

The next few days were bitterly empty for Daniel's father. He was away from the house a lot.

Christy spent much of her time with her family. She had been praying for years for her brother, Ken. He had never accepted Jesus as his Savior. Ken had proclaimed being agnostic for most of his adult life. One morning he and Christy were talking about the service. He was very impressed with the outpouring of love for Daniel. Ken said that he wasn't ready to accept the idea of Jesus being the Savior of the world, but that he had definitely felt something during the service and he would pursue seeking the truth. They had a good long discussion about Daniel's faith and she got to share the gospel with Ken through Daniel's life. Christy was elated that Ken was open to even discussing the possibility of Jesus as Lord.

Jamie enjoyed spending some time with her cousins. She hadn't seen them in over a year. It helped having family around.

On Saturday, Christy got a chance to spend some time with her sister Nancy. After some talk about their families, Nancy questioned Christy about getting rid of their newer cars and why they had moved to a smaller home. Christy took the opportunity to share about the 3t Challenge. At first, Nancy scoffed at the idea. But as Christy shared how much happier life was after taking the Challenge, Nancy seemed to be more interested. She eventually said she was going to talk with her husband about the idea. Nancy admitted that although they were regular church attenders, their walk with Jesus was very weak. Nancy said her family were all growing apart and she was getting worried about where they were headed. She and Christy had a good time of prayer after the conversation.

When Jamie wasn't spending time with her cousins, she was reading through Daniels journal and actively working on her laptop. Christy wondered what she was working so hard on.

She also wondered why her husband wasn't around much at all.

Sunday morning Pastor Patrick woke up and got ready for church, just like any other Sunday. He told Christy he was the preacher and people expected him to be at work. She had replied that she and Jamie weren't in any condition to go yet. They were still grieving the loss of Daniel. He seemed to be moving on. He acted energetic and ready to preach. Christy worried a lot about this decision. When she tried to talk to him about her feelings, he basically shut her down. It reminded her of how he acted before the church fire last spring.

As Pastor Patrick entered Big Oak Christian Church, most people were surprised to see him. He spoke to many people who gave him their condolences. He walked up to Sister Snyder who was seated.

"Good morning, Sister Snyder!" He said enthusiastically.

She looked up at him surprised and said, "My word, Pastor. What in the world are you doing here?"

He answered, "Well, the last time I checked I was the preacher at this church."

Sister Snyder said, "Yes. Yes you are. But you have had a tragedy. You need time to mourn. Rushing back into the pulpit is not a wise decision."

He replied, "I'm fine. My son was killed. But he was a Christian. So he's in Heaven. He's better off than all of us. Right?"

Sister Snyder said, "Yes. He is in Heaven. But you aren't. And you need time to grieve with your family. I strongly suggest you turn around and go home. Your family needs you right now."

He said, "I'm ok. I promise. I've got to get going."

He hurried away to the stage. He greeted the worship band who were all surprised to see him.

He took the stage and welcomed everyone. He thanked them for their condolences and attending his son's funeral service. It was awkward how detached he seemed to be toward losing his son.

The worship band performed, but it was very awkward with Pastor Patrick unexpectedly there. Sky and Chloe performed well, but it was as if they held back due to the pastor's presence. Everyone just felt sorry for him.

He stood to preach. First, he began by bragging about how nice the new family life center was coming along. Then, he noted how envious other churches would be of Big Oak. He then proceeded to preach the most judgmental, hateful and angry sermon anyone could remember hearing. When he was finished and the service ended most people were in shock.

As Sister Snyder left she said, "Will I be seeing you on Tuesday?"

Pastor Patrick replied, "Sounds great!"

She turned and left without another word.

That afternoon, Christy insisted he stay home to see her family off. He finally agreed and asked Clint to lead the Sunday night gathering.

During the evening service, Big Oak Christian Church spent their whole time in fervent prayer for their pastor.

Chapter 38

Tuesday morning Pastor Patrick showed up at Sister Snyder's home just as he had so many times before. She let him in and went and had a seat.

She said bluntly, "What are you doing here?"

He was rather shocked and answered, "Well, we regularly meet on Tuesday's. And you asked me on Sunday if I was coming over. I said that I was."

Sister Snyder said, "Yes and that is a conversation that should never have taken place, because you should not have been there."

He flippantly replied, "I'm good. Life is for the living."

Sister Snyder answered, "You should have been with your family grieving the loss of Daniel."

He said, "Well, I don't see..."

He was abruptly interrupted by Sister Snyder, "Instead you were being self-righteous and preaching in anger. I've lived through this with my Seth and Timothy. I assure you nothing good will come of it!"

He asked, "Timothy? Who's that?"

Sister Snyder froze. She hadn't intended to bring Timothy into this. She slowly stood and walked over to the wall to her right. She removed a black and white picture of a small child. He had never inquired who the child was. He figured it was a picture of Seth when he was a baby or a nephew or someone.

She composed herself and explained, "Two years after Seth and I were married I became pregnant. We were elated. My father had decided to step down as pastor of Big Oak to plant two other churches. He was traveling every Sunday between them. Seth became the pastor of Big Oak at that time. He was the second pastor they had ever had. Those were some of the most wonderful times. I gave birth to Timothy who was such a lovely baby. He had the cutest little chubby cheeks. We delighted in everything he did. For the first two years of his life things were wonderful. Seth loved preaching and being a daddy. Then one morning I went to get Timothy up. He wasn't moving. Wasn't breathing. I screamed for Seth. We rushed him over to the doctor's house. He was gone. A perfect little boy one day. Dead the next."

Sister Snyder reached over to get a tissue to wipe the tears from her face.

She continued, "We were devastated. Technology wasn't much back then. We never found out why Timothy died. It tore us both up. But Seth did a terrible job of dealing with it. He tried to just put it behind him and press on. He said he had duties at the church and didn't give himself time to grieve. It was horrible. Six months of the angriest preaching I have ever sat through. Then my father visited and that Sunday afternoon he took Seth for a walk. I don't know what he told him, but Seth came back a new man. We took a month-long sabbatical and really renewed our relationship with each other and with God. I was never able to conceive again, but the Lord gave us peace. The church became our family. Seth became a much better pastor than he ever would have been without the pain of losing our son."

Pastor Patrick's eyes welled up as he said, "I had no idea. I'm so sorry."

Sister Snyder said, "It's tough losing a child. Burying them is one of the toughest things a parent can do. But handling it wrong makes the problem exponentially worse! You are a good man. But you are blowing it right now. You must face this situation and deal with it mentally and emotionally."

He sat in silence for some time.

He finally broke the silence and said, "I hate thinking about Daniel. I miss him so much. It literally feels like my heart is breaking when I think about him." Then the tears came and he said, "He was such a wonderful son. He deserved a long happy life! I should have protected him better. He was so good. I should have done something."

Then his crying became sobs and Sister Snyder could only make out the words "Why God? Why?"

Later that morning he went home to let Christy and Jamie know they were going to take some time off to heal.

The next month was a refreshing time for the Spakes family. They spent a week together out of town in a cabin. Jamie missed the first week of school, but they felt it was more important for her to get healthy than to rush right back into school life. They took photo albums and celebrated Daniel's life. At times they would be laughing hysterically only to be crying a little while later. It was a time of healing for all of them spiritually and emotionally. There were times it was difficult to pray, but they asked God to teach them through the pain. By the end of the week Jamie was ready to get back to school and see her friends.

Christy met with her women's Bible study. They were a great emotional help for her. Pastor Patrick visited Victor several times. Not to do any church planning, but to talk through his feelings and struggles.

When the month long sabbatical was complete the entire Spakes family was in a much better place mentally, spiritually, and emotionally. Pastor Patrick resumed his duties at Big Oak refreshed and excited about his relationship with God once again.

During his first service back he apologized to the church for "preaching angry" as Sister Snyder had put it.

Clint had done an amazing job filling in for him during his time away.

Sky and Chloe were about a month away from their wedding. They were excited, but worried their pastor might not be ready to perform the ceremony. He assured them he was very excited about performing their wedding and he wouldn't think of backing out. He also had a surprise for them. He was able to reserve "The Grove" in Lost Creek for the wedding. This was an area on a beautiful pond that was outrageously expensive to reserve. Pastor Patrick said he had received an offer from a friend to donate it if they wanted to be married there. They jumped at the offer.

Over the next month, Sky and Chloe's wedding was about the only positive thing going on. Big Oak had more sickness, job loss, marriage problems and deaths than the Spakes had experienced in their entire time in Lost Creek. The weather was wet and nasty almost every day. The family life center had unexpected complications and the completion date was moved back to the spring.

Pastor Patrick and Christy spent a lot of time counseling and encouraging church members.

They genuinely looked forward to evenings planning the wedding. It took their minds off the problems so many people were facing in their church.

He kept encouraging his congregation to be obedient to God and to trust in Him. Prayer services included more and more fervent prayer. Still some people began questioning God's faithfulness.

Sister Snyder told them God was allowing all of this pain to make the church trust only in Jesus. She explained the Bible teaches how the purest gold has to go through the hottest fire. God allows tough times to build tough people. Everyone was finding out this meek little old lady was still a valiant prayer warrior.

When the Saturday of the wedding finally arrived, everyone halfway expected it to be a washout. Miraculously it was one of the prettiest days anyone could remember.

Chapter 39

Pastor Patrick and Sky stood by the picturesque crystal clear blue lake with about one hundred and fifty wedding guests watching the glistening white horse-drawn carriage rolling toward them through a row of magnificently towering trees. If they didn't know better they would have thought this was a royal wedding or something straight from a fairy-tale. The open-air white carriage pulled up to the wedding party. Two ushers helped Chloe and her father out of it. A small string orchestra began to play the Wedding March. Sky stood a little bit taller today, Pastor Patrick thought to himself. Chloe was radiant in her beautiful white wedding gown.

Her father walked her forward and placed her hand in Sky's. He leaned over to Sky and whispered something. Sky nodded and said, "Thank you, Sir."

As the ceremony began, Christy thought about how miraculously this day had come together. A member of Big Oak called and wanted to donate this area in "The Grove" for Sky and Chloe's wedding. Then another man called and donated the horse and carriage. The string orchestra was the next donation. Then the food for the reception, the wedding cake, and the reception tent were all donated.

Finally, Pastor Patrick asked who was orchestrating all of this good-will. After some investigating he discovered Joe was behind it. He called him and asked him why he was doing all of this for Sky and Chloe. Joe told him he had simply called in some favors. Pastor Patrick pressed him on the reason for calling in the favors. Joe finally explained that after the accident he was broken in every way. He came to the end of himself and realized how wrong he had been. He shared he had begged God for forgiveness and even pledged to take the 3t Challenge. This is what came from that pledge. The men decided to meet and talk things out. It was a healthy meeting. They agreed Joe should come back to Big Oak and they should continue to meet together.

Pastor Patrick was going through the vows. Tears were rolling down both of the young couples cheeks.

Jamie was thinking how much Daniel would have loved being here today. She had read in Daniel's journal how much he respected Sky for saving himself for marriage. Chloe had encouraged Jamie to also stay pure.

119

Finishing the ceremony Pastor Patrick said, "I now pronounce you man and wife. You may kiss the bride."

They shared a long romantic kiss.

As the orchestra began playing he announced, "Ladies and Gentlemen, I am proud to introduce to you Mr. and Mrs. Sky Burleson."

It was as if on the day of the wedding a curse was lifted from Big Oak Christian Church. Two new companies moved into town and hired a lot of the jobless people. The health of the congregation began improving dramatically. The family life center was coming along nicely and looking great.

Big Oak began having two morning services and was continuing to grow. Pastor Patrick had begun a pastor's prayer group with several other leaders from Lost Creek, Westside, and the capital city. Most of them had offered the 3t Challenge to their congregations with great success.

Pastor Patrick had some wonderful visits with Sister Snyder. He was amazed at how much wisdom he always gained from his time meeting with her.

Victor and New Hope had almost tripled in size since the great revival. They were having multiple services to accommodate everyone. With so many people looking for ways to serve God with their time, talents, and treasures ministry opportunities were being met every day of the week.

Jamie finally revealed what she had been so actively working on for the past few months. She had taken Daniel's journal and made a daily devotional Bible study from his writings. It incorporated Daniel's thoughts, ideas, and stories with scripture. She had done a wonderful job putting it all together. Pastor Patrick and Christy were so proud of her. He promised to help her get it published.

The anniversary of the big church fire was coming up this Sunday. Pastor Patrick was reviewing his sermon late Saturday afternoon when he got a phone call.

He hung up and walked into the living room where Christy was.

He said, "Honey, it's Sister Snyder. Dr. Johnson says she's not well."

Christy replied, "Oh no! I hate to hear that. You said she was looking weak yesterday. Do you want me to go the hospital with you?"

He said, "We're not going to the hospital. She's refusing to leave her house. Christy, I'm afraid her time is very short. He said to hurry."

Christy jumped up and said, "Let's go!"

They arrived a short time later. There were some ladies from the church already there. Dr. Johnson was there with his wife.

Pastor Patrick asked him, "How is she, David?"

Dr. Johnson replied, "Not good, Pastor. She's very weak and her heart rate is slow. It doesn't look good at this point. But, hey, I learned a long time ago not to write off this woman of God!"

Pastor Patrick smiled thinking back to the miraculous recovery of Sister Snyder less than a year ago. That event led to a great amount of faith building in many people's lives. Dr. Johnson was saved just after it. But the Lord was not leading him to pray for her recovery this time.

Pastor Patrick said, "Thank you, David. May we see her?"

Dr. Johnson said, "Yes. You better get in there. She's been asking for you."

He and Christy entered Sister Snyder's bedroom. He noticed a picture of Seth and Timothy on her nightstand. Sister Snyder was on her back with her head propped up.

She weakly said, "Don't you two have a better place to spend your date night than here?"

He smiled. He took Sister Snyder's hand and said, "This is cheaper than a movie."

Sister Snyder laughed lightly and said, "Ms. Christy you married a big spender didn't you."

Christy laughed and said, "What he lacks in spending, he makes up for in spontaneity. I had no idea we would be seeing you today."

Sister Snyder said, "Pastor, I don't know what you did to get such a catch, but you're one lucky fella. You better cherish this one."

He replied, "I do. Very much."

Sister Snyder said, "The Lord told me I'll be seeing Him soon. I'm so ready. I can't wait to see my Seth and Timothy. I can't wait to see my Jesus. But I am glad God allowed me to see you grow into the man you are today. You are a fine pastor. Keep loving those people."

He said, "You have blessed my life more than you will ever know. I wish I had realized how special you were earlier in my ministry at Big Oak."

Sister Snyder said very softly, "Now don't go talking about regrets. God's timing is perfect. Are you still going to announce our little secret tomorrow?"

121

He smiled and said, "Yes. Just like we talked about. I wish you could be there."

Sister Snyder was sounding weaker. She said almost in a whisper, "I will be...in spirit"

He replied, "Sister Snyder. Thank you for being faithful to Jesus. I love you."

Sister Snyder was quiet for a time. Her breathing slowed.

Then she said, "It is well...with...my soul."

She squeezed Pastor Patrick's hand a little tighter and then gasped one last time. Her grip went soft.

In an instant she was gone from this world into eternity.

Chapter 40

Pastor Patrick Spakes looked across the sanctuary filled with more people than its pews could hold, and he was filled with humility. All of the praying and fasting, encouraging his members and inviting those without a church home was rewarding. He was glad he had learned to keep a healthy balance between ministry and family. There were so many people they ran out of chairs. He looked out into the congregation and smiled at his lovely wife, Christy. She was sitting with Jamie as always. She smiled back thinking how happy she was to be his wife.

Sky and Chloe had just finished the invitation and the congregation was basking in the love of the Holy Spirit. This was of great concern to Pastor Patrick. Success or failure would be determined this morning by people experiencing God.

Alvin and Missy Bond were visiting on this day with their baby boy. Everyone was glad to see them. Earlier in the service, Alvin had shared how his church had offered the 3t Challenge and some of the major changes people had experienced.

After the morning sermon, he invited those who wanted to publicly accept Salvation to come forward. He prayed silently, "Lord, I know you are in control. Thank you for allowing me to share the Truth with all of these people today. Please be with those making decisions now."

God was answering his prayers.

As people made their way back to their seats, Pastor Patrick stepped up and said, "It's been a wonderful morning Big Oak. I have one more thing to share with all of you. As you know the family life center will be opening up next week. The finishing touches will be done by Friday. We will have a ribbon cutting service, followed by a prayer service on Saturday at noon. As I shared in my sermon, one year ago this week was a life changing time for me. God's love ripped through my pride and God used a fire, a health scare, and a little old lady to bring me back to Him. Many of you have suggested we name the new building in honor of my son, Daniel. I'm touched and honored by your thoughtfulness. But I believe there's a more appropriate name. The Church Council and the Board of Deacons agreed unanimously. Next week Big Oak Christian Church will open the Snyder Family Life Center. Most of you knew Sister Snyder personally. Some of you knew Seth Snyder, who was the second pastor of Big Oak for fifty years. But not many of you, if any, knew Timothy Snyder, Seth and Elizabeth's son. He tragically passed away at the age of two. Though Seth and Sister Snyder were devastated, they tried to have more children, but weren't able to. So they adopted the people of Big Oak as their family. I can't think of a more appropriate name than the Snyder Family Life Center.

I spoke with Sister Snyder about this before she passed away. She said it was an honor to know her family would always be remembered by Big Oak. I told her that Big Oak would not be what it is today without the Snyder family. And that is the truth.

We will celebrate Sister Snyder's life at her funeral here tomorrow at two p.m. I know she has influenced most of you here today. She impacted my life greatly. She is a woman who walked with God. She gave her time, talents, and treasures to the Lord long before we coined the phrase '3t Challenge'.

God received the first fruits of her life. May we all love God and love people the way she demonstrated for us."

Pastor Patrick bowed his head, prayed a powerful prayer, and dismissed Big Oak Christian Church to go impact the world.

The End

Epilogue

Five years after the great church fire, Big Oak Christian Church is still going strong, pastored by Pastor Patrick Spakes. They have a Saturday service and three services on Sunday mornings. The gatherings on Sunday nights are still incredible and the 3t Challenge is still being taken and changing lives. Big Oak has planted and supports four other churches in and around the capital city. Pastor Patrick is careful to protect his time with his family and friends.

Jamie and JJ Smith went to the same college and fell in love. They have been married for about a year. He is in his first year of seminary and she is an acclaimed author. The devotional she wrote using Daniel's journal turned out to be a best seller. She is currently working on a novel about Sister Snyder's life.

Sky and Chloe are still leading worship at Big Oak. They have a two year-old son and are expecting a daughter any day now. They recorded a worship CD and had a single that Sky wrote get as high as number three on the Christian music charts.

Christy's brother, Ken, eventually accepted Jesus as his Savior. He is currently happily married to a wonderful Christian lady.

Christy's sister, Nancy, and her husband took the 3t Challenge. They have never been happier.

Clint O'Dell moved to the west coast and became a lead pastor. He's doing great and stays in touch with Pastor Patrick.

Pastor Victor Martinez and Maria have three kids. All girls. New Hope Church acquired a larger building, but still uses the one by the school for the after school program.

Dwayne leads the after school program for New Hope. Theresa married and moved out of state. She stays in touch with Jamie regularly. Julius is an ordained minister working in the capital city.

Hector and Elizabeth had two more sons. Pedro is getting big. They all attend New Hope and are a great help to Victor. Hector still considers Pastor Patrick his pastor, but he loves serving with Victor.

The 3t Challenge had a major impact on the community. Thousands of people have taken the year-long challenge and changed the way they use their time, talents, and treasures. The crime rate in Lost Creek, Westside and the capital city is down. The teenage pregnancy rate, drug use and divorce rate are also exponentially down. Church attendance is up. Politicians, community leaders, and activists have all tried to take credit for lowering violence and raising morality.

Pastor Patrick just smiles and gives God the credit when asked his opinion.

He regularly visits Daniel, Sister Snyder and Joe Smith's graves. Joe died about two years ago of cancer.

Joe once said it was amazing to see what God can do when ordinary people give their first fruits to God. Pastor Patrick couldn't agree more.

A Note to the Reader about Salvation

I hope you enjoyed the book First Fruits. Although this a fictional book, the principles are based in truth. As pointed out several times throughout the book the 3t Challenge is about people's stewardship to God, not their Salvation. Without Salvation, the 3t Challenge is worthless.

We all need to be saved from our sins. The Bible says that every person has sinned (Romans 3:23). It goes on the say, while we don't deserve Salvation, God offers it to us as a free gift (Romans 6:23). In fact, while we were enemies of God and living in sin, God sent His only Son to die for us (Romans 5:8). God did this because He loves us so much and we can receive eternal life with God by believing in His Son Jesus Christ (John 3:16). We show evidence of this faith in Jesus by believing in our hearts and confessing with our mouths that Jesus is Lord (Romans 10:9-10).

While it is not a part of our Salvation, the very first thing we're supposed to do to when we are saved is to be baptized (Romans 6:4-5). The next step is fellowship with other believer's and growing spiritually.

God loves you no matter how bad you think you are. You are not too far gone for Jesus to reach out and save you. Call out to God, turn from the direction you are going and follow Him.

You can do that right now in your own words if you like. If you need someone to talk with or are interested in learning more about what it means to have a relationship with Jesus Christ, a great resource is 1-888-Need-Him (1-888-633-3446). Or on the web, go to www.needhim.org. You can also chat with someone about what a relationship with Jesus is all about at www.chataboutjesus.com. I pray you will acknowledge Jesus as your Lord and receive Salvation today!

The 3t Challenge for You

Just as Pastor Patrick issued the 3t Challenge to his congregation, I would like to offer it to you. If you are a Christian, God is calling you to follow Him. The 3t Challenge is simply spending your time, talents and treasures the way the Holy Spirit leads you. Remember we aren't saved by our good works. The 3t Challenge is a practical way to follow God after we have received Salvation. Sometimes it helps to write things down to remind us of our commitments. Below is a commitment pledge you may want to sign to remind you of the Challenge you are accepting. Please pray about this and don't take this pledge lightly.

"I will, to the best of my ability, serve God with my time, talents, and treasures for the next year. I acknowledge that only the free gift of God's grace can save me. This is an expression of my desire to follow God with what He has given me. Through prayer and obeying Biblical principles I will trust God to lead me as I strive to follow Him."

_____

Name

_____

Date

Helping You Succeed with the 3t Challenge

How can you use your TIME more efficiently for God? What can you sacrifice to spend more of your time following Jesus?

How can you creatively use your TALENTS for the Lord? Everyone has abilities they can use for the Kingdom. What are yours?

How can you spend your TREASURES in a better way for Jesus? What are some innovative ways you can give to the Lord?

A word of encouragement for you:
God has created you just the way you are for a very special purpose that only you can fulfill. God loves you and wants you to live an abundant life. It may not always be easy to follow Him, but ultimately it will be worth it! Trials and temptations will be tough, but God is bigger and better than any obstacle you may face. Fight the good fight and keep your journey on the straight and narrow path. God loves you so much that He sent His Son to die for you. The Gospel will see you through.

For more information on the 3tChallenge please contact:
www.3tChallenge.com

Discussion Questions

Chp 1 What do you think is Pastor Patrick's basic problem? Contrast "pride" and "gratefulness." Do you struggle with pride? If so, how do you deal with it?

Chp 2 If someone you knew walked up to you and said, "I have a word from the Lord for you," how would you respond? Read 1 Corinthians 3:11-13 and Exodus 23:19 and discuss them.

Chp 3 Pastor Patrick incorrectly concluded Sister Snyder did not like change. Discuss why he probably thought this. Why do people struggle with changes in church?

Chp 4 Have you ever faced disaster? What lessons did you learn?

Chp 5 What are your thoughts on Sister Snyder advising Pastor Patrick to listen to God instead of answering his question herself?

Chp 6 Pastor Patrick had a renewal of his faith and intimacy with the Holy Spirit. How would you describe your understanding and relationship with the Holy Spirit? How did Pastor Patrick's renewal of faith affect his family?

Chp 7 Pastor enlisted a mentor and prayer partner, Sister Snyder. Do you have a weekly mentor or prayer partner in your life? What are your thoughts on having these in your life?

Chp 8 Pastor Patrick issued the 3tChallenge. What is your initial reaction to this challenge of giving God your time, talents, and treasures?

Chp 9 Following God led to adversity in Big Oak Christian Church. Have you had to deal with adversity in friendships or in church? What did you learn?

Chp 11 Pastor Patrick had mixed reactions to the 3tChallenge. Why do you think the reaction was mixed? Do you see the 3t's in operation in our churches? If more people applied them, what would happen in your church and community?

Chp 12 How do you see Big Oak Church applying the 3tChallenge here? Was this out of their comfort zone?

Chp 13 What did Pastor Patrick recognize Victor needed? He led Victor back to his experience of when he first encountered God. What can you remember of your first experience with Christ?

Chp 14 Explain Pastor Patrick's assessment of the Hope Center. How has his perspective changed from earlier?

Chp 16 Obeying God sometimes does require sacrifice. Can you recall a time when you had sacrifice for God?

Chp 18 Pastor Patrick shares some practical ways to honor God through the 3t's. Are you able to identify with any of these? Can you see the movement of God through Buzz's obedience? Have you ever been energized by God through someone else's obedience?

Chp 20 Discuss what God asked Pastor Patrick and his family to do.

Chp 21 How did God honor Pastor Patrick's obedience in this chapter? A key to living an abundant Christian life was mentioned as being obedient to Christ. Do you struggle with obedience to what you know God is leading you to do?

Chp 22 Were disagreements handled properly in this chapter? Have you ever had to use Biblical reconciliation in a situation?

Chp 24 All 3t's are seen in this chapter. Which of them would you have been involved in if you were a member of Big Oak?

Chp 25 Do you have any friends who culturally or financially different from you? Do you think it's important to have diverse friendships?

Chp 26 Victor stated he could see a difference in those taking the 3tChallenge. Pastor Patrick shared God had opened his eyes to his own complacency. Are there any areas in your life where you feel complacent?

Chp 27 Sister Snyder experienced a major miracle. Do you think God still does miracles today?

Chp 28 Have you ever been involved in collective prayer time for something specific? Describe the situation and what happened?

Chp 30 Julius asked, "Is there any hope for me?" How would you answer him?

Chp 31 "What's impossible for us is possible for Jesus!" Have you ever faced something impossible and saw Jesus come through?

Chp 32 "Many were moved by the Holy Spirit." Have you ever been moved by the Holy Spirit? If so, how were you changed?

Chp 34 After a day of victory, tragedy strikes. Have you experienced an emotional ride like this? What did you learn from it?

Chp 35 "Whether, then, you eat or drink whatever you do, do all to the glory of God." (1 Cor. 10:31) What are your thoughts about this scripture? Daniel said in his journal, "I should live on purpose for Jesus." What does this mean to you?

Chp 36 "How great is our God?" Can you share anything about how great God is to you?

Chp 38 Have you ever cried out to God, "Why?" What was your answer?

Chp 40 Compare the heart of Pastor Patrick and Big Oak Christian Church in this last chapter with the first. Our 3t's bathed in prayer, with foundation of the gospel is what God uses to change lives. How will you respond to giving God your time, talents, and treasures?

35078035R00084

Made in the USA
Middletown, DE
18 September 2016